W9-APE-774

PICKLE
The (Formerly) Anonymous PRANK CLUB of
Fountain Point Middle School

Kim Baker

Illustrated by Tim Probert

Roaring Brook Press • New York

To Jack and Molly. And to mischief makers everywhere.
This one's for you.

Published by Roaring Brook Press
Roaring Brook Press is a division of Holtzbrinck Publishing Holdings
Limited Partnership
175 Fifth Avenue, New York, New York 10010
mackids.com

Library of Congress Cataloging-in-Publication Data

Baker, Kim.
PICKLE : the (formerly) anonymous prank club of Fountain Point Middle School / Kim Baker. — 1st ed.
p. cm.
Summary: Using a bogus name, the League of Pickle Makers, sixth-grader Ben and three recruits start a prank-pulling club and receive funding from their middle school's PTA.
ISBN 978-1-59643-765-4 (hardcover)
[1. Practical jokes—Fiction. 2. Clubs—Fiction. 3. Middle schools—Fiction. 4. Schools—Fiction.] I. Title.
PZ7.B174297Pi 2012
[Fic]—dc23

2011045402

Roaring Brook Press books are available for special promotions and premiums. For details contact: Director of Special Markets, Holtzbrinck Publishers.

First edition 2012
Book design by Andrew Arnold
Printed in the United States of America by RR Donnelley & Sons Company, Harrisonburg, Virginia

10 9 8 7 6 5 4 3 2 1

1 Top Secret

Can I trust you? I mean, to tell you this story I need to know that you can keep a couple of secrets. I'm already in a whole lot of trouble, and it's not just me. But I want to tell you everything that happened. Everything. I'll assume that you can keep the important stuff secret and not pass this book on to anyone older than twenty. I've been paying attention, and I'm pretty sure that's when a person's sense of humor starts leaking out. If somebody is that old, this isn't their kind of story, anyway.

I'm talking about the League of Pickle Makers. Can you think of a club a person would be less curious about? That's the point. Five of us meet on Thursdays, after school in the science lab. You'd expect somebody would think it was fishy that a group of kids are excited enough about making pickles to meet every week. On meeting days we take turns making a show out of carrying around some vinegar or a sack of cucumbers. We even have a website. Check it out—www.pickles forever.com. Click on the "Fizzy Pickle Soup" recipe, and then click on the word "simmer" down at the bottom. The password is "cheese."

Now you know we're not really an organization of picklers. Honestly, I don't even like pickles that much. Only a few people know how it all started. Us—and if you think you can handle it—you.

2
The Balls

One day after school, I looked through the online classifieds while I waited for my best friend, Hector, to get back from shoe shopping with his grandma. Finn Romo had told Hector and me that he found a practically new skate ramp in the free classifieds the week before. Someone just gave it away. I didn't believe him, so I walked over to his house to check it out. It wasn't that big, but it still took up the whole yard. The plywood wasn't even scuffed. Hector and I live in the same apartment building. We don't have a yard, so a ramp wouldn't work, but I wanted to see what other stuff people were just giving away. There were some cool things. Somebody was trying to get rid of a ferret named Bill, and someone else was giving away a unicycle with a sparkly red seat. I thought about emailing them, but something else caught my eye. Pete's Pizza, the local pizza place with all the games and stuff, had a post for free ball-pit balls for anyone who would come pick them up. The post said the balls were free "as is." I dropped a blue raspberry slushy in the ball pit at Pete's when I was five, and I know Katie McLeod's little brother puked in there at his birthday party, so I had a pretty good idea what "as is" meant. Still, *free!*

Hector had been flaking out a lot lately, so there was only a fifty/fifty chance he'd even want to hang out when he got back to our building. I called the pizza parlor. The guy who answered said the balls would go to the first person who came and got them. So I grabbed a couple of black trash bags and ran down to Pete's Pizza like my butt was on fire.

For future reference, there are more than two bags of balls in a ball pit. A lot more. It smelled funky, but I still took a few bag-filling breaks to jump around and do some belly flops. Pete asked me how long I was going to take, so I filled up the second bag, ran home, and stashed them in my bedroom. I grabbed a box of garbage bags on my way out and made six more trips. I'm not going to lie: the closer I got to the bottom, the dirtier the balls got. I found a purple earring, two different sets of keys, three half-eaten lollipops, more than a few pizza crusts, and a copy of *A Cricket in Times Square* with a ripped cover.

I think Pete was getting pretty tired of me carrying bags of stinky balls out of his pizza parlor, because he said I could use the safety nets around the pit to haul the rest of the balls. After I scooped out the very last ball, Pete gave me some free pizza, like I'd done him a favor.

It was a really big pit. My bedroom was full after the first twelve bags, so I left the nets in the living room.

I didn't really have a plan for what I would do with the balls, so I figured I'd watch some TV until Hector got back. My dad came home just as *Best Bloopers* ended, and the first thing he said was "What's that smell, Ben?"

I told him about the major free ball score, but he didn't share my enthusiasm.

"You can't keep them here" was the second thing he said. Did I mention that my dad is over twenty, and therefore has sprung a humor leak? He walked around the apartment opening windows. "Get rid of them. It smells like a Parmesan cheese factory in here."

"I think they smell like feet."

"Parmesan cheese smells like feet," he said. He was right. But I didn't think I could take the balls back to Pete. I had eaten the pizza already, so it felt like a done deal. He might not be happy to see me back, and Pete's a big guy.

"You can't keep them here. *Comprendes?*" My dad said. When he starts out in English and ends in Spanish, he means business.

I thought about just dumping the balls straight out of our living room window so they would roll down the street. We live on a pretty big hill, and a million balls bouncing and rolling away would be something to see.

But it would be less than awesome to clean up the balls, or have cars crash when they got pummeled with giant colored hail. The police might not like it, and I'm pretty sure Pete would rat me out if they started asking questions. For a guy who runs a pizza place with video games and stuff, he doesn't seem crazy about kids. I got a jolt like I had slammed an energy drink and I knew what I could do.

"I'll take care of it," I said, and headed the six blocks back to school.

The school was still open for clubs. Hector and his grandma were in the front hall talking to Leo Saylor and his dad. Hector held a bag from the Shoe Station. I couldn't see what kind of shoes were in the bag, but I could guess. Hector's grandma usually picks his shoes out. They never have shoelaces, because she doesn't want him to trip. They usually have Velcro straps, and thick heavy soles that are supposed to keep his spine straight, or something.

I ducked behind the big fountain in front so they wouldn't see me. I was on a mission.

Hector's grandma is the principal, which is why Hector *always* stays out of trouble. I thought about getting his attention and filling him in about my ball plan, but I knew what his reaction would be. He looks like a tough guy, but having the principal for a grandma has done something to his nerves.

Our homeroom is around the back on the first floor, so it was easy to scope out. It was empty, and the windows were open. Perfect.

I went straight back to my apartment for the bags. My dad was watching a movie in the living room, so I dropped them off of the fire escape as quietly as I could. If I wasn't gone by the time the movie finished, he would ask where I was taking them. I heard the end music just as I climbed out of the window. I carried the bags back down the hill to our school and stashed them in the bushes under the windows. Then I ran back for more.

I was on the last trip, carrying one of the big nets full of balls over my shoulder when I smacked into Leo's dad, coming out of the school. Mr. Saylor is huge, so I almost dropped the balls all over the sidewalk. He talks a lot about how he played football and water polo in college, and I believe it. Leo is in soccer, junior baseball, young golfers, wrestling, and basketball. He falls asleep in class sometimes.

I started to fall, but Mr. Saylor grabbed my shoulder. It was dark out by then, so I hoped he wouldn't be able to see well enough to recognize my face. I thought about running away, but Mr. Saylor held on to my shoulder with he-man strength.

"Easy, Ben," he said. So much for nonrecognition. He smiled at me and glanced down. "Some sort of game tonight?" In the dark, the net just looked like an equipment bag.

"Yeah. Game," I said. I held my breath and waited for him to ask what sport Leo wasn't playing yet.

"GO BEAVERS!" he shouted, and walked past me down the sidewalk.

I ran back to the classroom window and started throwing balls in like I was warming up for the mound. I might play more sports if they were as exciting as this. It gave me goose bumps, and I may or may not have been laughing like a lunatic all by myself.

I could have stayed there all night, throwing them in one by one, but I had to get back home before my dad freaked out. I poured the rest of the bags through the opening, and then it was done. I shut the window so everyone would be more confused about where the balls came from, but the smell sticking to my hands was already grossing me out. I didn't want to sit in a class that smelled like that tomorrow, so I reopened it. I couldn't see into the classroom very well, but it looked like the balls were pretty deep. I just stood there taking it in until I heard footsteps. I ducked into the bushes and Leo and Hector walked by. I worried that they had heard me giggling to myself and would investigate, but they didn't. I stayed hidden until I heard the gym door slam and the night was quiet again.

In the Morning

I woke up about ten times that night to check the clock. It felt like the balls were bouncing around in my stomach, but in a good way. I got dressed before my mom finished making her morning coffee and went downstairs to grab Hector. He sat waiting for me in the hall outside of his apartment, with his breakfast on a paper towel in his lap. Hector had been on the dried fruit and protein bar train for a while. He held a brown rectangle out to me.

"It's a date bar. My grandma made them. Want one?" he said. I took half of one and jogged down the sidewalk. "Dude, why are you going so fast? We're going to be early."

"I'm just in a good mood," I said.

"I was in a good mood until I tasted this date bar. Yech." He shook his head. I nibbled the corner off of mine. It tasted like peas, even though I couldn't see any green stuff in there.

We stopped at the bodega for *pan dulce* and orange juice to wash the taste out of our mouths.

"Come on, Hector!" I held the door open, but he'd stopped to check the baseball scores in the paper.

"What's the hurry?"

"I just don't want to be late," I said. He looked at me like I was crazy, but he put the paper down and followed me out. I tried not to walk too fast, but it was hard.

Ms. Ruiz keeps the classroom locked, and she doesn't come to open the door until the bell rings. I bounced from foot to foot while we waited in the hall and Hector talked about some shark show he'd seen on TV. I spotted Ms. Ruiz down the hall. She seemed to be dragging her feet even more than usual. There are posters up all over our room saying things like "Excellence Through Determination!" with marathon runners and rock climbers, but the posters are the only enthusiastic thing I have ever seen about Ms. Ruiz. I could have crawled to the classroom faster than she walked.

The bell rang just as she finally stopped in front of the classroom door. It's like she timed it precisely so she wouldn't have to get there a second too soon. She opened the door, and a couple of the people closest to the front of the crowd gasped. Everybody got quiet, beholding the awesomeness. The balls sat in a pile three feet high under the windows. They were spread across the floor, under desks, all the way to the other wall. The open windows hadn't done much for the stench.

"It's like one of those ball crawls!" Hector said. I raised my eyebrows and made my eyes big, which hopefully looked like surprise. Then everybody was pushing into the room at once and the smell didn't stop anybody from diving in. We jumped around like a bunch of sugared-up four-year-olds. A few kids ran around kicking balls. Frank Lenny grabbed a couple of balls and started juggling.

Finn yelled, "Ball fight!" And then it got really crazy. Balls were flying everywhere. Maggie

Rubio did a belly flop and hit her head on the math center. Bean Lee pulled her camera out and started filming a video. I whacked Hector in the stomach with a dented green ball.

"Cut it out! That hurt," he said. He rubbed his stomach with one hand and threw a ball at Bean Lee with the other. I know I didn't hit him that hard, but I apologized anyway. I definitely did not hit him as hard as he hit me in the eye a minute later. He didn't say he was sorry, he just laughed.

Ms. Ruiz called someone on the phone, and I tried to read her lips to see if it was Principal Lebonsky. I'd passed her in the hall on the way into class, and she did not look particularly happy. Not that she ever did. Even when she was smiling it was more like she was just showing her teeth. Frank grabbed three more balls and tried to juggle five at once. Ms. Ruiz hung up and yelled, "Everybody just calm down." She watched Oliver Swanson lie down on his stomach and pretend to swim through the balls across the room. Then she gave up and sat down at her desk. I kind of wanted her to freak out a little bit more, but I guess freaking out is not her style. A ball landed smack in her coffee and she pulled it out and chucked it back onto the floor. Then she yawned and took a drink. Yuck.

I ducked a flying red ball and kept an eye on the door. I was waiting for Principal Lebonsky, but Rick the janitor opened it. Rick came in, muttered something that sounded like "Sweet cheeses," and left. He came back with a box of trash bags and handed one to each kid without a word.

"Come on, man! Just let us have a few more minutes," Oliver said.

"Why don't we ask Principal Lebonsky if *she* thinks you should have a couple more minutes," Rick said. We started scooping, even though I think he was bluffing. He didn't want to talk to her any more than anybody else. I've seen the look on his face after she's told him to clean the toilets.

Even scooping up the balls was fun. Everybody got into the cleaning. Except Maggie. She played the head-injury card and sat down at her desk while the rest of us scooped. Ms. Ruiz said she had to go back to the teacher's lounge for a few minutes. Kids tried to throw balls into other kids' bags across the room until Rick said to cut it out.

"Did you do this?" I asked everyone, just in case anyone suspected that it had been me. I made a let-me-in-on-the-joke face. The other kids wanted to know how the balls got there, but nobody had a clue. By the time Ms. Ruiz got back with a new mug of coffee, the leading theory was that some seventh- or eighth-grade criminal mastermind was behind the whole thing. I just nodded and tried to keep all the happy I was feeling on the inside.

We set the bags of balls out in the hallway for Rick, and Ms. Ruiz started a lecture on Greek myths. I drew balls and stars in my notebook while she wrote names of Greek gods and goddesses on the whiteboard. Then I passed Hector a note.

THAT WAS AWESOME!!!

He nodded and tucked the paper into his notebook. Then he got it back out and scribbled something down on it.

I wonder what's going to happen next.

4
Character Building

"We should try something like that," I said when Hector and I were alone on the way home after school.

"Like what?"

"The balls. Something fun." Hector picked up a crumpled soda can and threw it into a trash can fifteen feet ahead of us. It didn't even touch the side. Usually when he makes a great shot, he'll make a whoop, or a fist pump or something. He just put his hands in his pockets and kept walking.

"Nah. I can't."

"What? Why not?"

"Because, dude. Whoever put the balls in there is going to get into trouble. My grandma heard about it from Rick. She asked if I knew who started it, and if I 'participated in the foolery.' "

Hector made quote marks with his fingers, but I would

have already guessed that those were Principal Lebonsky's words, and not his.

"What did you tell her?"

"I said I didn't know who put them there, and I didn't throw any."

"What does she think, you just sat there at your desk taking notes while everybody else goofed off?"

"I don't know. Whatever. If I told her I'd been playing around she would have given me a character card."

It sounds like something from a game, but it's not. Principal Lebonsky gives Hector a yellow index card with an inspirational quote anytime she doesn't like something he did. Sometimes the quotes are from Thomas Jefferson and people like that, but most of the time it's stuff she made up. He has to tack them to his bedroom door. Once he gets up to five, bad things happen. Last time, she took his skateboard for two weeks. He tried to tell her that skateboarding is exercise, but she doesn't think it counts.

The worst thing is nothing good happens if he doesn't get cards. He just has to wait until he messes up somehow, and more cards come.

"Those cards are dumber than dog sweaters," I said.

"Yeah," was all Hector said.

"Maybe I'll do something. Like, on my own. Then you wouldn't get into any trouble, but it would still be fun."

"Sure," he said, but his eyebrows were all squished

together. I wondered if he would tell on me and get me busted. He caught me looking sideways at him. "I'm not going to rat you out." He looked offended, like he'd read my mind, and I felt like a lowly worm. Then he added, "I mean, I probably won't." The guilt left and I shoved him.

"Dude! You do *not* know what she's like," Hector said. He was wrong—I did. It was bad enough before, when she was just my friend's grandma in the building, but since we started at Fountain Point, she's our principal, too. Still, unless she slipped truth serum into Hector's buckwheat spaghetti or something, he could try a little harder to keep a lid on it. I didn't talk to him the rest of the way to my parents' restaurant.

"I wouldn't, you know. Tell. If you wanted to do something like the balls," he said. "I know you're still mad about the last time." His voice was real low, as if his grandma trailed us down the sidewalk.

We were both thinking about The Graffiti Incident.

Last summer, right before school started, someone wrote "Principal Doodyhead Lives Here" with some really bad stick figures in fat, permanent marker all over the back door of our building. Hector told his grandma about it. Mistake #1. She asked Hector if he did it. She'd put him on a diet the week before, so he might have been my first guess, too. He swore he didn't, so she kept questioning. She asked if I did it. Hector said no at first, he swears, but she said if he didn't start telling the truth he'd be eating salad for a month. Green stuff is his kryptonite.

He told her we'd done it together. Don't ask me why, I guess he just panicked. He knew I didn't do it. As if we would write something so dopey on our own building! Principal Lebonsky made us spend the afternoon painting the door. AND she gave us lunchtime detention for our whole first week of middle school, even though we didn't get in trouble there. It made us look like pretty tough sixth graders, but still. I used to like her. I used to call her Betty. Now, even though she's my best friend's grandma, I call her Principal Lebonsky. She hasn't asked me to stop.

I could tell you about a few other times when Hector spilled his guts. Like when he ratted Bean out for sticking gum under the table at the beginning of the year. But The

Graffiti Incident was the big whammy. I never really thought that Hector could've done it, and I'm pretty sure he knows me well enough to know that I didn't do it. But, that didn't stop him from telling his grandma that I did. Hector sold me out for something I didn't even do the second his grandma put the squeeze on him. And, yeah, I'm still mad about it.

"I know you wouldn't tell, Hector. Thanks." I felt, like, eighty-seven percent sure. "I've gotta go to work."

We said goodbye, and I went into Lupe's and worked until closing because one of the busboys didn't show up.

5 The Stink of Room 121

After a couple of days, the whole school seemed to be waiting to see what might happen next. I went online to check out the free classifieds for inspiration, but nothing jumped out at me. This time it was mostly old carpet that somebody's cat peed on and stuff. There's nothing funny about that, even with the stink factor.

When you search online for pranks, it's mostly the same ten or so on a bunch of different sites. I learned that high school kids do a lot of the same tricks again and again. Most of them involve fake poop, burned football fields, or numbered farm animals. I don't know where these schools are, but there aren't a lot of sheep in the city, let alone any you can paint. Before I fell asleep that night, I knew two things. I needed a plan. And if I wanted to do something big—maybe even bigger than the balls—I probably needed some help.

By Monday, everyone in the whole school had heard about the balls. Even though only a little bit of the smell stuck around, Room 121 officially became known as the "Pit of Stink." Some kids said it like we were the worst sixth grade homeroom, but I think it made Room 121 sound like there was a mysterious adventure happening.

Principal Lebonsky made the morning announcements herself. She did the one-two-three-eyes-on-me claps that she always does, even though she was in her office where we couldn't see her and it was just her voice blaring out of the classroom speakers. After the parts about the lunch menu and some pioneer thing, she cleared her throat.

"I wish to address the monkey business in Room 121 last week," she said. "Any further mischief will not be tolerated. While the stunt with the balls might have been a temporarily amusing lark for some, please remember that student creativity should be confined to the traditional arts. Or music. Practical jokes toy with the molds of good character. I know this will be the end of the matter. Thank you."

It was like a dare. Kids were more interested than ever in the Pit of Stink. Everybody asked everybody else if they knew anything about it. People wondered if it might have been an inside job from somebody in our homeroom. I asked people, too, and said over and over how awesome and genius it was—but just to throw off suspicion—not like I'm conceited.

6 The List

"Oliver did it," Maggie Rubio whispered the next morning. I looked at Oliver, sitting two rows over. We watched him doodling lightning bolts on his notebook, and I wondered what he had done. Maggie likes to accuse people of randomly selected, gross bodily functions, stuff even I don't like to talk about. I gave her a vague nod and waited for the handouts to come down the row. You couldn't be rude about it, because then you might be the next kid who "did" something. "The balls, Ben. Oliver's the one who brought the balls on Friday." She gave him a look like he invented root beer floats, and then she had my attention.

"What do you mean he brought the balls? He told you?"

"He didn't have to. I asked him and he just smiled and shrugged, but you could totally tell that he was the one who did it. Isn't that wild?" I almost contradicted her and confessed, but I didn't need her giving *me* a weird dreamy look like that, so I kept my cool. Oliver looked back at us and smiled.

Maybe Oliver would be good to team up with, but it would probably be better to recruit a couple more people. I still didn't know that many kids at Fountain Point, but when Maggie got up to give a report on Pandora's box I made a list of the kids I did know with a good sense of humor. I put a star by the name of anyone that had something special, like a history of causing trouble or a knack with computers.

Hector's name sat at the top of the list. He's my oldest friend, *and* he has access to the keys to the school. He sat right beside me fiddling with the corner of his notebook, the way we'd been sitting for years. I glanced over, but he wasn't paying any attention to me. He took notes on what Ms. Ruiz was saying about flying horses as if he were about to get one for a pet. He didn't know I was thinking about how we walked to school together, and we walked home together. Hector noticed me looking at him and tried to flick me in the temple with his pen, but I ducked out of the way.

I drew a line straight through his name and then another zigzag line over that.

I knew that I didn't want Hector in the group, but once I admitted that Hector wouldn't be my partner in crime I felt bad even seeing his name there. And I didn't want him to see it, either.

But, The Graffiti Incident was a problem. It effectively disqualified Hector from any plans that would need to be kept secret. He couldn't keep a secret with a mouth full of pudding.

I crossed out a few more names, leaving only two kids that met my requirements: Oliver Swanson and Frank Lenny. Oliver already claimed responsibility for the balls, and he once convinced half the class that his real parents had found him and he was going to live with them on a submarine. Frank Lenny owned a computer, could fart at will, and had an obsession with ninjas. He went to a different elementary school than I did. I heard he went to a few different ones. I didn't know him, but I wanted to. He always seemed cool and private. And sometimes, he hung out with seventh graders.

Oliver and Frank seemed like cool dudes, and with my idea for a secret prank task team, I knew they would want to join forces. Here were two guys who could make awesome buddies and probably have the natural talent for supreme goofing off.

I needed them on my team.

An Invitation

After math I grabbed the bathroom pass and left class as coolly as I could. I slid notes into Oliver's and Frank's locker through the vents. The lockers were on different sides of the school, so I had to run to get back to class before they noticed that I was gone too long. I'd practiced writing them over and over in block letters until it didn't look anything like my handwriting.

The notes said:

FOR YOUR EYES ONLY!

DO YOU HAVE AN APPRECIATION OF PRANKS? WOULD YOU LIKE TO BE A SECRET AGENT?

MEET ME AT LUPE'S AFTER SCHOOL TOMORROW TO HEAR MORE.

TELL NO ONE.

The Meeting

I waited in the back booth of the restaurant, where I do my homework sometimes after school. The restaurant was a tomb—apart from the mariachi music that Diego, the cook, played in the kitchen. The front door swung open and flashed sunlight onto my table.

It was Oliver. He stood there for a minute, looking around, but I don't think he saw me.

"Are you looking for Ben?" my mom asked.

"Oh . . . all right. Sure."

"He's in the back."

Oliver walked toward my table. "Hey. What's up?" he said.

"Thanks for coming, Oliver," I said. "I wanted to congratulate you on the balls in the classroom. That was super."

"Oh, thanks." He studied the painting over the booth. It

was an old lady with flowers in her hair, and it wasn't that interesting.

"Where'd you get them?" I asked.

"Where did I get what?"

"The balls. Where did you get so many balls?"

"Oh, right." Oliver cleared his throat. "I just found them somewhere." My mom walked back into the kitchen, so I dropped my voice.

"Uh-huh."

"Okay, I didn't really. It wasn't me."

"I know," I said.

"How do you know?" he said. My mom came back out of the kitchen, so I just smiled. Oliver looked confused for a minute, and then I could tell the lightbulb flickered on.

"Sweet." He nodded and sat down. "Is that what this is about then? Something like that?"

The front door bells chimed. The door opened and closed again quickly.

"Is Ben here?"

Frank. Somehow he'd figured out that I'd put the invitation in his locker. My mom pointed toward us and he walked slowly back. He wore mirrored sunglasses, like a cop or a biker, and he didn't even take them off inside the restaurant. My mom and dad keep Lupe's pretty dark for romantic dates . . . I expected Frank to bump into something. He didn't.

Frank nodded to Oliver, and then to me. He sat down at our booth, sunglasses still on, and slid the invitation facedown across the table.

"I got your message. I like your style. It looks like you've done your research. You want someone familiar with the inner workings of the human mind. Someone who can make things. Fix things. Know things." Frank tapped his temple. "You're assembling a team, and you want the best. Congratulations. I'm here, and I'm listening."

"How did you know I sent the invitation?" I asked.

"You said to meet here. This is your family's restaurant." Frank took off his sunglasses and squinted at each of us. We stared back at him.

Diego brought some guacamole and chips out and slid them across the table. "Your mom thought you guys might need some snacks," he said.

"Thanks, Diego," I said. He went back into the kitchen and sang along with gusto to some song about a mean redhead running away with his heart and horse. I hoped that Oliver and Frank didn't know Spanish.

Oliver dug in and Frank waited for him to stop crunching before he spoke again. "What can I do for you?"

"Yeah, Ben." Oliver glanced at my mom and leaned forward. "What is this about?"

"I'm making a secret society for pranks and goofing off." I tried to keep my voice as low as possible. It sounded kind of cool. "The Pit of Stink? I did that." Frank's eyes flicked to Oliver, and then back to me. "I'm ready to do more, but I can't do it alone. I think you two might be able to help." Oliver smiled and nodded, but Frank stayed still. A loud motorcycle went by, and Diego chopped in the kitchen.

"Who else have you asked?" Frank said.

"Yeah, who else knows about this?" Oliver said.

"No one," I said.

"What do you have in mind?" Frank asked. "I gotta tell you, fake dog poop and trick gum aren't really my thing."

"Nah, I don't want to do stuff like that. I'm talking about big stuff. The ball pit could be just the beginning," I said. I noticed my hands were shaking a little, so I put them under the table. "I want to have fun—but it has to be secret. Which means *no* bragging." I looked right at Oliver.

"Cool," Oliver said, and took another chip. We waited for him to eat it. "What? I didn't tell anybody I did the balls. I just didn't tell them they were wrong when they thought I did."

"Well, you can't do that, either. It's got to be our secret," I said. "You have to swear."

"Fine," Oliver said. "I swear."

"You'd better," I said. "Nobody can know."

Frank put his sunglasses on and stood up.

"I think I understand," he said. "I'll be in touch."

"Don't tell anybody," I called after him. My mom didn't turn around, but she sat up straighter in the universal position of parental eavesdropping. There wasn't anything left to overhear because the bells jingled over the door and Frank Lenny was gone.

My mom was still listening so I gestured to Oliver and we left, too. Once we were out on the sidewalk, he turned to me.

"Do you think he'll tell?"

"I don't know," I said. I was wondering the same thing. "I've only known him this year. I heard this is, like, his sixth school. We don't even know anything about him." Oliver stopped walking, and he looked a little ticked.

"Some kids move. It doesn't really have anything to do with them. You know?" he said. "They just go where the grown-ups tell them to go. It doesn't mean he's a kid superspy or anything. It just means people move him around."

I remembered too late that Oliver knew something about moving around. Before he got placed with his "forever family," as his parents said, he'd been to a few foster homes. I remember the day he moved in down the block. I was skating in front of our building when a man in a suit the color of green olives walked Oliver past and into a doorway with a black awning on the corner. Oliver carried a trash bag full of clothes. He looked like he was in trouble. Oliver told me later that he'd used that same bag to carry his stuff from two different families. The first people decided they didn't want to foster a kid anymore, and the second family got pretty mean until Oliver told his social worker.

"You're right. I didn't mean . . . Sorry," I said. Oliver shrugged and we walked down the block. "UNLESS, he's really a thirty-year-old baby-faced CIA agent undercover at Fountain Point to bust . . . Mr. Roberts for an illegal gambling ring. Maybe they're taking bets on how we do on our spelling tests."

"Interesting theory, Ben," Oliver said in a way that sounded like it was definitely not an interesting theory. "We'll just have to wait and see."

A Side of Bean

After school the next day on my way to Lupe's, Bean Lee jumped out from behind an alley trash can. She wore red overalls with "Stand Back" written on the front pocket.

Bean is kind of famous, in an Internet way. She started that Cat vs. Dude site with the cats fighting action figures and stuff. And you should know that Bean has more than one pair of red overalls. She has another pair with a patch of a panda bear playing drums, *and* some green ones with holes in the knees that she wears striped tights under. She wears a blue feather boa sometimes, and she's sewn animal ears onto most of her hats and hoodies. You'd think it would be easier to see her coming, but she made me jump. She makes me jump a lot.

"Mr. Diaz, we have an important matter to discuss."

I'd passed Bean digging around in her locker when I left school, so I don't know how she beat me to the corner. The way she acted made me think it had something to do with Frank. Plus, they hang out together a lot. And I heard he helped her set up www.catvsdude.com. "My associate would like to accept your organization's offer . . . with stipulations."

"What associate?" I said. I tried to look confused.

"Are you organizing a prank task force or running a bad acting club?"

I shrugged. Bean stared me down.

"My little sister does a better job playing dumb. I know everything. Our mutual friend is willing to join forces—with conditions." She crossed her arms, and we had some sort of silent standoff. I think she tried to tell me to chill out telepathically, but I wasn't ready to give in. It could have been a bluff. She waited for me to slip up and tell her everything. I made a face that said I had no idea what she could possibly be talking about, but it only lasted about ten seconds.

"Fine. What kind of conditions does Frank have?" I said. Bean cracked her knuckles and smirked.

"Number one. If Frank's in the club, your friend, Mr. Junior Principal, is not," she said. "Actually, that one is mine."

I could have told Bean that Hector wasn't invited, but I didn't like her bossing me around.

"Listen, Bean, I—"

"NUMBER TWO"—Bean held up her hand to shush me—"I, too, am interested in joining. You can have us both, or neither." She stuck her chin out and stood tall, but she was still a foot shorter than me.

"No way," I said. "I get to pick who's in the club. Besides, he wasn't supposed to tell anybody. He already broke the rules."

"I'm not just anybody. And I am a crack-proof safe for secrets," Bean said. "Plus, Principal Lebonsky and I aren't exactly on the same side."

"The, um, club is by invitation only. Sorry, Bean." I was only sorry in a feeling-a-little-bit-guilty way. Not a regretful way.

"Okey dokey, artichokey. I'll let Frank know that you're not into it." She skipped back toward the school. I felt relieved that she'd given up so easily. It started dawning on me that it might have been *too easy*, when she stopped and swiveled back around. "Too bad. We could have done a lot with the costumes."

"What costumes?"

"The ones in my dad's shop, silly. Lee's Costume & Party? It could have been kind of super."

So, then there were four of us.

A Cryptic Message

I checked my email in the morning. And then I called Oliver.

"Frank is like a super spy," I said after Oliver let me have it for waking him up.

"What? Why?"

"He just emailed me! He's never emailed me before. And I've never emailed him! I checked. How did he get my email address? Do you think he hacked my computer?"

"I think he used the roster they gave us at orientation," Oliver said, and hung up. That bummed me out a little bit, but then I opened the email and it was in Japanese. I didn't even know Frank knew Japanese, and I don't know why he thought I did. I called Oliver again.

"It's not even in English," I said.

"What's not in English?" Oliver said in a deep, slow voice.

"Did you fall back asleep?"

"Yes."

"But we were just on the phone, like, a minute ago."

"So?" he said. "I was up late rehearsing for *Hello, Dolly!* The spring play? I have the lead, you know."

"You're Dolly?"

"No! I'm Horace Vandergelder," Oliver said.

"I don't know what that means."

"What do you want, Ben?"

"Well, I opened Frank's email. It's in Japanese or something. Why does he think I know Japanese?"

"That sounds like a question for Frank," Oliver said. Then he hung up again.

I found the school roster in the junk drawer in the kitchen and called Frank up.

"Hello, Ben," Frank answered. "You have questions about my message."

"How did you know?" I said. I heard Frank yawn.

"What can I do for you?"

"Well, you know the email you sent? It looks like it's in Japanese. I don't really know Japanese, so I wondered if you could, like, send it in English?"

"I don't know Japanese. Neither do you. Neither does Ms. Ruiz, Principal Lebonsky, or most anybody else in our school. In case your email has been compromised," Frank said. While he talked my computer beeped and another email popped up from an Agent Fix-it with a link to an online email language translator and a note:

`Next time it might be in Russian.`

"Whoa. Who's Agent Fix-it?" Maybe Frank had invited someone *else* into the club.

"That would be me," he said, and hung up.

So cool. I translated the email that Frank sent, and it turned out to be a paragraph cut and pasted from the Board of Education website. It said that any student could form a club at school by telling the head office. If the office accepted the group as a legitimate organization and it had four or more members, it qualified for special funding from the Parent Teacher Association (P.T.A.).

We had a group of four students, but it's not like we could go tell them that we wanted to cause trouble. We needed a cover. If we started a secret club and called it something else, something innocent and non-suspicious, we could meet at school and they'd give us money.

Double identities!

I opened a new email account under the name Agent Queso (my cheese love knows no bounds) and forwarded the email to Oliver (in Turkish), with the link to the translator.

Do you think we should start a club at school? Use the translator to respond.

Then I called him again.

"I just wanted to tell you that you have an email," I said. "It's from someone you know, but with a fake name."

"Okay."

"It's from me." He didn't say anything. "Did you hear me, or did you doze off again? I sent you an email."

"Cool. I'll go read it." Oliver yawned. "Anything else?"

"Nope, that's it. I just wanted you to read your email," I said.

"Okay, if I need to write you back it will just show up in your email and you can read it when you want to. I'm not going to call you or anything."

"All right."

I started to say how cool it would be to have double identities when I realized that he had hung up on me again. I went back to the computer to wait for his email. I think he went back to sleep again, because I didn't get anything until lunchtime. Under "*Do you think we should start a club at school?"* Oliver had typed one word.

Sí.

He put the link to the translator on the bottom.

11 The Club

I stopped in the office after school to ask for the form for a new club.

"Are you starting a new group?" Pat said. She's the school secretary and she looked as if a new club would make her day. I'm pretty sure she has more Fountain Point sweatshirts than anyone else at school. The office also has about a dozen beaver figurines on the windowsills. I don't think they're Principal Lebonsky's.

"I think so," I said. "I mean, I'm thinking about it."

"Maybe someone's already formed a group that matches your interests, Ben." She gave me a bright orange sheet of paper with a list of all the student organizations already at Fountain Point. She smiled and nodded, so I smiled and nodded, too, but that was weird so I looked down at the form. She kept standing there, like she couldn't wait to see my eyes sparkle with glee when I saw the perfect club met on Mondays or something. I read the list. Fountain Point Middle School has a lot of groups. They called them "Extracurricular Enrichment Opportunities." Whatever. Basically, there are art- and gym-type things. Everything from chess club to rugby. Really. Jack MacDougal's dad is from Scotland and he started a team. I don't know who they play.

The most popular clubs on the list were the soccer team, dance squad, science club, the Beaver Band, and Oliver's beloved drama club—those I already knew about. The graphic novel club sounded cool. There were a few wacky ones, like a lassoing team. We lived in the city, not the Wild Wild West. What did they lasso—pigeons? The list said they currently had eight members. Sounded fishy to me. Maybe they were some sort of secret club, too.

After a minute, when I didn't jump up and down, Pat gave me the new club application form and another bunch of papers. Then she went back to her desk and took out a sack lunch.

The first two pages were the Fountain Point Middle School Group Code of Conduct Contract (F.P.M.S.G.C.C.C.). Pat told me I had to put my initials after each rule to show that I'd read it, and then sign the bottom. There were *a lot* of rules, in really small print. I didn't read all of them, but I skimmed it. A couple of weird ones popped out, like the group couldn't be about overthrowing the government. And each group needs a board with a president and stuff. The last rule said that Fountain Point had a zero-tolerance policy for any groups that Principal Lebonsky deemed "destructive, disobedient, or overly disruptive."

I initialed everything and started on the application. I filled in the blanks as best I could with my name and stuff. Then I got to the "prospective group description."

Maybe, if you started a club at school, you would have it be a Dog Appreciation Society or Happy Cookie Bakers or something. But I needed to come up with a club that other kids would not be interested in, but adults would believe that kids might find interesting. Tricky.

I looked around the office for a clue. Paper clips. Paper clip collectors? No. Fluorescent light lovers? Vintage copy machine appreciators? I tried to think of something, anything that would make a good club, while Pat picked the pickles out of her tuna salad sandwich. Copy machines might have potential. Hector and I tried to make copies of our squished faces once while we waited for his grandma. I forgot to close my eyes, and I couldn't see anything but green blobs for three hours. The copies turned out kind of cool though. I still have them taped up on my closet door.

"Nobody likes pickles this much," Pat said under her breath. I don't like pickles much, either, so I gave her an I-heard-that look. She flicked pickle discs into the trash like tiny green Frisbees. I looked back down at the form. It became so clear what the club needed to be, it was as if the paper in my hands had turned green. I thought about it for another minute, but I couldn't think of anything better. This would be perfect.

The League of Pickle Makers was born.

I knew kids wouldn't try and join a club for pickles. Hector wouldn't be interested, either. He's hated pickles ever since he got sick from a bad egg salad sandwich.

I signed us up for a weekly meeting and put everybody's name down under the board of directors.

PRESIDENT: Ben Diaz
VICE PRESIDENT: Frank Lenny
SECRETARY: Oliver Swanson
TREASURER: Bean Lee

I felt goofy putting myself down as president, but it made me kind of happy, too. I'd never tell Bean she was treasurer. Ever. I gave the form to Pat, and she looked it over.

"Oh, honey. I'm sorry I said people don't like pickles." She looked worried that I might be offended by her pickle dissing. "I should have offered them to you, but they had tuna juice anyway, and my husband just buys whatever is on sale. They weren't made from scratch or anything."

"That's okay," I said. "Pickles aren't for everybody."

She told me that someone would be getting in contact

with me about the club, and that she would make a note that I was the pickle president.

I can think of a million things I'd rather be known as than the pickle president. And I don't think Oliver, Frank, or Bean would call me president even if I held them down and moved their lips. But maybe the rest of the school would. I have more than two years left at Fountain Point. President Pickle is something that could stick with you all the way to high school. Maybe I should have started a weight lifting team.

I recognized this as the first test of my new, double identity. Did Clark Kent rip off his glasses and tell the world he was Superman? Did Bruce Wayne take the Batmobile to pick up groceries? No, they did not.

"The other kids won't have to call you President Diaz or anything. It's just for the form," Pat said.

" 'President Diaz.' I like the sound of that," I said. "All right, just on the form, though. I think all of the pickle makers should be . . . equal." It sounded kind of corny, but Pat looked proud. I left the office while the getting was good.

Service with a Smile

There were a lot of reservations that night at the restaurant, so my mom and dad both had to work. I asked if I could stay home and watch TV, but they said no. We all headed to Lupe's together.

"We'd just rather have you here with us at night, *m'ijo*," my mom said, and handed me a clean apron.

"It's a lot of responsibility to be home alone at night," my dad said. He left the kitchen, and I rolled my eyes at Diego. He stopped stirring the *posole* to raise his hands in surrender. He'll listen when I gripe about my parents, but he won't commiserate with me. Diego's not the kind of guy to complain about his bosses. I went back out into the dining room to find my mom. She was talking to some customers in the front booth and waved me over when she saw me. I didn't see who it was until I was there. Principal Lebonsky and two other principal-looking ladies.

"Good evening, Ben," Principal Lebonsky said. "I was just asking your mother if it would be possible to have an order of more . . . traditional enchiladas." My mom laughed like she does when the health inspector makes a bad knock-knock joke.

"You know, Betty, we've always made our enchiladas that way. It's a custom I learned from my grandmother and *tías*. An old family recipe," my mom said. She is a little sensitive about the food at the restaurant, and a lot sensitive about family. Our enchiladas come with green chile and a fried egg on top. It's the way our family has always made them. And, by the way, they are perfection.

"I've just never seen them prepared in such a manner," Principal Lebonsky said. She wasn't saying it like it was cool that my mom did it like that, more like that Mom was wrong to do it differently from what the principal was used to. It was the same way she talked to the kids at school. I wanted to tell them to go eat somewhere else for dinner. Or I wanted my mom to refuse to serve her. Sure, it would be a little extreme, but it would also be totally aces. But, my mom just got her pad and pen out and smiled at them. I stood behind Principal Lebonsky and made a face, but my mom wouldn't look at me.

Principal Lebonsky decided to go with a taco plate instead, and the other ladies ordered fajitas. My mom asked me to take their food out when it was ready. I started to say no, but she stopped me with a look and I nodded. It worked out better for me if they weren't buddies. She said I could keep the tip, which made it better.

"Ben is one of my students at Fountain Point. He has promise, but disciplinary issues," Principal Lebonsky told the other ladies when I cleared their plates. Like I wasn't even there. And I don't have "disciplinary issues." The only time I've had detention is for The Graffiti Incident—and that doesn't count because a) it wasn't me, and b) it didn't happen at school. I noticed my mom watching from the kitchen door, so I just put the bill down and walked away from the table.

"Don't stay here too late, Ben. Remember, it's a school night," Principal Lebonsky said when she came up to the register to pay the bill.

"Oh, I'm going home soon," I said. Then I thought she might offer to walk me back to the apartment. "I mean, after I help take out the trash and stuff. And I already did my homework for tomorrow." I thought that would earn me some points. It didn't. She only left me ten percent.

A Twist in the Plot that Could Not Have Been Foreseen

"Did you think I wouldn't find out, Ben?"

The next day, Ms. Ruiz asked me to come back after school for a quick chat. "*You* have been up to something," she said in a singsong voice.

I'd been a little jumpy ever since gym class. Rick gave Coach Capell the balls from the Pit of Stink to recycle in P.E. He told us to play dodgeball with them because it would be "mellower" with the little balls. It wasn't so bad until he went to make a phone call. A couple of guys got tennis racquets out of the equipment room to lob the balls harder. There wasn't anything mellow about the whizzing rainbow of pain. And I didn't think the gym could smell any worse, but smacking those balls around really released the aroma. When Coach Capell came back he said we had creativity. I think he meant we had welts.

"So, Ben. I hear you want to create a special team," Ms. Ruiz wiped off the whiteboard. Were we busted already? "I have to say, it's not what I'd expect from you, but I'm intrigued. What a creative idea. Think of the possibilities." Her eyes were sparkly and she looked a little breathless. Oh, man. She knew. She totally knew.

"Um, yeah, possibilities," I said.

"What made you think of doing something like this? Have you been practicing at the restaurant?"

"No! I wouldn't do anything like that in the restaurant."

"I bet you'd have a lot to work with there. Your parents might be able to give you some ideas, too," she said. I highly doubted it. I didn't know how much she knew, or where she heard it from. Obviously, somebody talked. I took a shaky step backward and sat down in a chair.

"Who told?"

"The office told me what you were up to this morning," she said.

"The office knows?" It felt like there was a blender in my chest. I ran my hands through my hair and tried to come up with an explanation.

"If you don't mind, I have a request. I would like to be your faculty advisor." She waited for me to respond. "For the *League of Pickle Makers*!"

"Oh! Oh! Great," I said. They didn't know anything! But, I might have underestimated pickle popularity.

"Don't worry. I won't interfere," she said. "Too many cooks spoil the stew, right? Or should I say too many cloves ruin the brine!" She laughed. She laughed alone. "Do you have a preference for a day to meet?"

"Thursday, please. Sometimes I help in the restaurant other days, but Thursdays I always have off," I said. She wrote something down on a sticky note.

"I tried to have you meet here in the classroom where I could help a bit when I finished lesson planning, but Principal Lebonsky is worried that it might be messy and there could be more lingering smells. She's asked that you meet in the second floor laboratory." Ms. Ruiz pressed her lips together until they disappeared. "So, just be responsible and clean up after yourself in the lab, and you and I can meet once in a while to talk about your pickling plans." We sat there, and I could tell she wanted me to say something. I tried to come up with something nice to say about pickles, but she couldn't wait that long.

She smiled at me like she had just inherited a candy factory. A big one. Or something else that teachers are into, like a dry-erase marker warehouse. "I know what you're planning."

I studied her face again. She was definitely excited about something. I couldn't remember the last time I saw Ms. Ruiz get excited about anything. My mouth felt dry, and it made my lips stick to my teeth, which probably wasn't so bad if it kept me from talking.

She reached into her top right drawer and pulled out a sheet of butter-colored paper. She slid it across the desk facedown.

"Well, Mr. Diaz. Why don't you tell me what you know about *this*?"

I took the paper. Maybe I could shove it in my mouth to stop myself from confessing everything. I turned the paper over. It said:

PIONEER FAIR

Settler Reenactments, Real Livestock,
Demonstrations & Historic Snacks

Competitions! Fun! Games!

Saturday, April 21

11–3

Fountain Point Middle School

Come one, come all!

I looked at Ms. Ruiz.

"Don't play coy, Ben. The teachers have been planning it for a year. I called the planning committee last night. They confirmed that there would be a pickling and preserving competition, and I just knew that's why you started the group." I stared at her. "You can tell me, Ben. I'm your advisor. You and the League of Pickle Makers are planning on entering the contest, aren't you? You must have your eye on the cash prize."

I nodded.

Ms. Ruiz whooped and slapped her desk. I'd never seen her move so fast and it made me grab the arms of my chair. "I *knew* it. What are you planning? Traditional sour dills—or something more avant-garde—gherkins, maybe? Fountain Point is hosting the event, so many of our own groups and clubs will participate, but students and faculty from all over the district will be attending as well." She made a note to herself on a sticky pad and scratched her temple. "Oh, I almost forgot. You'll need this." She opened another drawer in her desk. "I brought you a cookbook from my *personal* collection and a little club funding to get you started." She handed me a huge, old book and an envelope.

"Okay, thanks, Ms. Ruiz. We're . . . really excited," I said.

"Of course you are." She clapped her hands together and we both looked down at the book in my hands.

The Joy of Pickling.

The cover had a couple of brown stains, and it smelled

like dust and garlic. She waited for me to open it, so I did. The pages were yellow around the edges with notes written in the margins. And lots of sticky notes. One recipe for pickle slaw had a note with three frowny faces, but most had stars and hearts. Ms. Ruiz made a lot of pickles. I wish I'd known that before I made us a pickle club. "I'm sure you'll find the perfect recipe to wow the judges," she said.

"Thanks, I'll, uh, take good care of this."

"I know you will, Ben. I know you will. Have fun. We'll have our first check-in soon."

I thanked her again and left. I stopped in the hall to inspect the envelope. It said:

Ben Diaz, President, League of Pickle Makers

Inside were two twenties and a ten.

Fifty bucks! We were rich!

14 The First (or Second) Prank

I got nervous that Ms. Ruiz would pop in on our first Thursday meeting to talk pickles, so I spent about half the money on three pounds of cucumbers and four jars of pickling spices for each of us to bust out if anyone started asking questions.

I thought they'd be mad that I'd already spent some of our club funds, but Frank said, "Good thinking." Oliver and Bean nodded.

We decided that we'd take turns bringing something pickle-able to the meetings in case Ms. Ruiz or Principal Lebonsky came by to see how we were doing. Nobody knew what else went into pickles, so we looked through *The Joy of Pickling*. The only other thing was vinegar, unless they were some sort of special pickle. That book had recipes for watermelon rinds, ginger, fish, and all kinds of stuff. There was even a recipe for pickled pigs feet. For real. I am not even making that up.

"Okay, Ben. You bring a big bottle of vinegar on Thursdays. Make sure to carry it around a lot so everybody sees it," Frank said. I thought maybe I should remind him who the president of this league of pickle makers was and suggest one of *them* carry a jug of stinky stuff around.

"Shouldn't we try actually making something?" Oliver said. "For the Pioneer Fair?"

We found a recipe for "Simple Pickles" in the front of the book. Oliver remembered that he'd seen some vinegar in one of the cupboards left over from the baking soda volcanoes in science class, and Frank scrounged up some jars. We threw in the cucumbers and a jar of the pickling spices and shook it up. Contest entry. Done!

"Let's talk pranks," I said.

"I know what we can do first," Bean said.

"The Pit of Stink was first," Oliver said, and Bean rolled her eyes.

"As a club, doofus," she said.

"You know, Bean, to be frank—"

"Don't try to be Frank. He's right here, and he's made out of magnificent. You are no Frank," Bean said. Frank nodded and Oliver rubbed his eyes.

"To be *honest*, people would like you more if you didn't call everyone names all the time," Oliver said.

"You're the one trying to be Frank," Bean said. I stood up.

"What's your idea, Bean?"

"Thank you, Ben." She shot a look at Oliver. "My idea is super simple. Minimal supplies, low risk, maximum impact, high visibility." She sounded like the guy who sold my mom her old station wagon.

"Suds, gentlemen. One bottle of dish soap in the fountain and we have a mountain of bubbles. I can't believe nobody has ever done it here before. My cousin Ted did it with his fraternity at college, and it was *A*-mazing. He posted pictures online. I saw."

Fountain Point was renamed after they built a fountain in the front. It was the Millard Fillmore Middle School before that, but he wasn't even a very good president. Some artist who grew up around here built the fountain and donated it to the school. It looked like it should have been in a park in Paris, not in front of our school. I mean, come on, naked babies sitting on pillars constantly pouring water out of big ugly pitchers? Their arms would be hurting something awful to have to keep holding the pitchers up like that. It's like baby torture. Don't tell anybody, but it creeps me out.

"That's actually a great idea, Bean," Oliver said. "What if we got two bottles and loaded up the drinking fountains, too?"

"Spectacular," Frank said. I thought about the babies pouring bubbles instead of dirty fountain water. We toasted with our pickling spice jars, and made plans to meet behind the bushes near the fountain after dinner. Bean offered to stop at the store for the dish soap, so I gave her five dollars of the club cash.

After dinner I loaded the dishwasher without being asked. When I was finished, I asked if I could go down to Oliver's apartment. Timing is everything.

"Sure, but just for a half an hour, okay?" my dad said. I left right away. I heard a birdcall when I got close to the school. Then I heard it again. And again. It was Frank. Frank and Bean were indeed waiting with Oliver in the bushes. Bean showed me a new bottle of green dish soap. It guaranteed softer hands after you cleaned with it. That might work on parents, but they needed to think of something better than soft hands to get kids to wash dishes. Bean climbed out of the bushes and walked out into the open. Frank and Oliver followed. Bean held the soap up near one of the fountain lights so we could all see the "Extra Suds!" sticker. The lights were bright enough for someone walking by to see us.

"Maybe this is a bad idea," I said, looking over my shoulder. "This seems more wrong than the ball pit." The fountain was huge, and out in front where the entire school would see it. And what if the soap broke the motor or stained the creepy babies or something?

"What's the big deal? It is just soap, Ben. It'll wash right off. The fountain will be cleaner than before. It's not like there are fish in there or anything," Bean said. I checked, but all I could see were old leaves, chewed gum, and pennies.

"What if we did that instead? That would be kind of cool if the fountain was suddenly full of goldfish! Everybody would be like, hey, where did they come from?" Oliver said. He looked kind of dreamy until Bean said they'd get sucked through the pumps. Then *she* looked kind of dreamy.

"It doesn't really take four of us to pour soap into a fountain," I said. It was true. "What if one of the teachers walks by? Or Principal Lebonsky? You can totally see us from the sidewalk." I know Principal Lebonsky takes a lot of evening strolls.

"Aren't we doing this as a club? Relax. Nothing really happens until the soap gets swished around. But in the morning, it will be everywhere." Bean didn't care if I freaked out or not. Maybe if I said not to do it, she would take Frank and start another prank club without us. She took the cap off and looked up, waiting for me to whine some more. I didn't.

"You guys have to promise not to tell anybody—about this, the club—anything," I said. They promised and I made Oliver swear, since he had fake-bragged about the balls. "We should probably set up some rules. Well, not rules, guidelines for the group and what kind of pranks we should do."

"Yeah, but later. You don't want to get caught, right?" Bean tipped the bottle and the soap glugged into the pool and sank to the bottom. It took a while to pour out, but it just stretched around the floor of the fountain like a green ribbon of goo. The last squirt left a trail of bubbles on the top, but nothing that would impress anybody. Maybe it wouldn't work after all.

"Why don't you get in there and swish it around? That might speed things up," Bean said. I took off my socks and shoes and rolled up my pants. I got into the fountain, and scooted through the cold, slippery piles of pennies. I sloshed my feet around, but it didn't really make any more bubbles.

"Try doing it faster," Bean said. I did, but the water just sloshed around and soaked my pants. I heard Bean and Oliver giggling, and knew I'd been had.

"See you in the morning," Frank said, and backed up into the darkness. Bean followed. I watched the green swirl around the bottom.

"Let's go, dude," Oliver said. "Someone's coming." I jumped out of the fountain and grabbed my socks and shoes. We ducked out of the fountain lights back into the bushes. We were totally hidden from the sidewalk, but anyone who stopped would see the tracks of my wet footprints leading right to us.

An old couple walked by, talking about whether they should throw a penny in the fountain and make a wish. The old man said he didn't have a penny, so the old woman asked him to check his pocket. Then she told him to check his other pocket. I worried that the fountain would start foaming up while they stood there looking for change, but after what felt like forever she believed him and they kept going down the sidewalk.

I got home with thirty seconds to spare.

Bubbles

I didn't see the fountain when I got to school. I didn't see it because it was covered in suds. A sparkly white pyramid stretched all the way to the top of the babies' pitchers. Some eighth graders were scooping out handfuls of bubbles and throwing them at each other like a snowball fight. Kids were trying to wrestle each other into the foam. A smallish kid I recognized from music class got pushed into the big jiggling mass of bubbles, and came out looking like a suds monster. Frank stood back with most of the rest of the school, admiring it from afar.

"Wow," I said.

"Pretty crazy," he said. "I wonder if there will be bubbles anywhere else today." Quick as a blink he flapped his coat open like he just needed to make an adjustment, but I caught a flash of green in his inside pocket. "I'll see you in class. I need to go get a drink first." Frank winked and cut through the crowd. I watched the bubble fight as more kids joined in. No matter how much they scooped out, it just kept growing. Hypnotic. I stood there until the bell rang.

Frank had been very, very thirsty. Bubbles grew in every drinking fountain on the way to class. That didn't stop anybody from pushing the silver buttons on the faucet to give them a little boost as they walked by. Each little squirt made the suds shake and grow, so that by the time I got down to my locker they overflowed and stretched across the floor. Rick stood at the end of the hall with his arms crossed beside the bucket and mop. He looked like a mad frog. Bean held her camera close to a drinking fountain and gave the button a couple of taps until the foam sloshed over the side.

"Margaret Lee. Come here." Rick never yelled exactly. It didn't even sound like he raised his voice, but he could be heard over a crowd of kids like that. Bean swung her camera away from the fountain, but she caught some suds on her sleeve. She stared at Rick, and he stared back.

She was busted and she knew it. Rick held out the mop. I really wanted to watch Bean try to clean up soap, but the late bell rang and I ran into class. Bean came back scowling forty-five minutes later and slammed into the desk behind me.

"How'd you clean up the foam so fast, *Margaret*?" I whispered over my shoulder. She leaned forward. "Don't. Say. It. Again." She smelled like dish soap.

"Say what? *Foam*? Oh, I get it. You don't want me to say *Mar*—ow, ow, OW! Fine." Bean wiggled her fingers and a few precious strands of my hair fell to the floor. I turned around to give her my dirtiest look.

"You know, you aren't really growing on me," I said.

"Sorry, sailor," Bean said. I looked at her a little closer as she worked out an algebra problem. I was surprised that it hadn't occurred to me before, but I realized that she totally didn't care if people liked her or not. Honestly, it made me like her a little more. I still needed to get her back for yanking my hair, though. That hurt.

I don't know what Rick did, but by the end of the day the bubbles were totally gone. I turned a drinking fountain on after school, and there were zero suds. I watched the water run down the drain like normal. Hector leaned over my shoulder.

"What are you staring at?" he said.

"What do you use to clean up soap?" I asked him.

"What is that, a riddle?"

"No, it's just a question."

"I don't know. Why don't you ask your new club?"

"What?" I turned around, but Hector had his head in his locker.

"Ab*surd* to *part a* stub." His voice came out muffled. It looked like he'd stuck his face into his backpack.

"Dude, I can't even hear you. What are you doing, sucking out crumbs?"

Hector leaned out and glared at me.

"I heard that you started a club," he mumbled.

"I did, well, Oliver and me. And a couple of other kids."

"From our building?"

"No, from school." My face felt hot, and I wished there was somewhere I needed to go. Anywhere.

"Uh-huh."

"I didn't think you'd be interested, so I didn't mention it," I said. Hector slammed his locker door.

"You're right. I'm not interested. What are you guys doing anyway?" My first instinct was to lie. I tried to think of something to tell him about what the club did, something he didn't like. I was close to saying the club made crossword puzzles or something when I remembered that we already had a cover.

"We're making pickles." There's just *no* way to say that and make it sound cool. Maybe crossword puzzles would have been better.

"Really?" Hector threw his backpack over his shoulder. I waited. "That sounds like the last club in the world anybody would join." He laughed and my stomach sank a little. I had my fingers crossed that he wouldn't ask to join, but I kind of wanted him to *want* to join. If he had, I might have said yes.

"Let's just get something to eat," I said.

"I'll meet you in the office," Hector said. He looked like he might say something else, but changed his mind.

Bolted

When I got to the office, Hector was already back behind the swinging doors talking to his grandma. She had her back to me, but I could see him squirming in his chair. He probably had to give her a minute-by-minute account of where we would be. I stayed put and studied the Pioneer Fair poster someone had hung up. It said "COMPETITIONS!" in big block letters in the middle. It said "Historic Snacks!" and "Livestock!" too, but "COMPETITIONS!" is what really jumped out at me.

I sat on the bolted-down wooden bench by the door, beside a girl I'd never seen before. She had a sour look on her face and crossed arms, and she smelled like carnations and cherry lip gloss. She glared at a woman writing at the counter. I tried to give the bench a subtle little shake with my butt, like I always do, but it didn't move, like it never does. The sour-faced girl, however, turned her head to give me a dirty look.

"Sorry. I wasn't trying to shake you. I like trying to shake the bench." Nothing. "Why do you think it's bolted down?" I talk when I'm nervous, and this girl made me nervous.

She didn't answer and looked away. I think it was her way of telling me to shut up.

"I mean, do you think it kept getting knocked over? I don't think so, because it seems pretty heavy." I tried shaking it again. Silence. "Do you think some dude just went totally nutso and tried to throw it? Maybe he just had too many detentions or something." I swallowed. "Or she. I don't mean to say that only a boy could lift up the bench. I know strong girls."

I know strong girls? Did that really come out of my mouth? Geesh. At least she didn't go to Fountain Point. She looked older. She definitely wore makeup. There was the lip gloss, and I'm pretty sure I detected some eyelash stuff. Other bits looked older, too. If she did go here, she'd be an eighth grader. Seventh grade, maybe, but probably eighth. She was probably just somebody's big sister picking them up for a doctor's appointment or something.

"So, just bring her birth certificate and immunization records with you on Monday and she'll be all set to start class, Mrs. Taylor—" Pat said.

"It's Ms., actually," the woman said. "We . . . well, it's Ms. Taylor now."

"Oh, all right. Well, Sienna's homeroom will be Room 121 with Ms. Ruiz."

Oh, crust. Pat took a closer look at the form. "Well look at that, dear! Monday's your birthday!" Pat said. She leaned forward over the counter. "If you'd like to have a special day and wait to start until Tuesday, that could be our little secret." Pat winked, but the girl's mom was already shaking her head.

"Oh, I'm sure Sienna will be eager to start school and get adjusted as soon as possible," her mom said.

Sienna didn't look like she wanted to get adjusted. She looked like she wanted to swing a bench. She stomped out instead and tried to whack the door against the wall, but they had something at the top of the door to stop that, too. It closed gently with a peaceful little *pffft* sound. I never noticed before, but it sounded kind of like someone farting. I giggled. Out of relief that the girl was gone, more than the fart sound. Her mom looked at me, and then I felt bad like I'd been giggling about her kid storming out, or something. I wanted to apologize for laughing, but she left before I could.

All right, that's a lie. She stood there for a minute looking more sad than ticked, but I didn't really want to tell her that it sounded like the door farted because that's just the kind of thing you might get sent to see Principal Lebonsky for, and I was already sitting right outside her office hoping she wouldn't notice me.

"Ben, can you come in here for a moment?" Principal Lebonsky called out. That's my luck for you.

"Did you see the fountain this morning?" Hector asked when I got there.

"How could I not see the fountain this morning?" I said. "It was incredible." Principal Lebonsky squinted at me. "Incredibly troubling, I mean."

"Do you know what happened?" she asked. I stood there not saying anything until Principal Lebonsky crossed her arms.

"It malfunctioned? Maybe?"

"Some reckless hooligans placed a great deal of detergent into the fountain sometime last night. I am curious to know whether you might have seen anyone acting suspiciously, or noticed anything different about the fountain. Did you?"

"I didn't see any bubbles until I got to school this morning," I said. It was literally true. I felt proud of myself and disgusted all at once.

"I wouldn't want to be them when they get caught," Hector said. I went with the truth again and said that I wouldn't, either. We stood there in silence until Principal Lebonsky sighed.

"I have work to do, boys. Please make sure and eat something healthy," she said.

"Let's go," Hector said, and he didn't have to tell me twice. We were out on the street in under a minute.

Hector wanted to go to Pete's Pizza, but I thought Pete might mention the balls. Or maybe Principal Lebonsky had already traced the balls back to Pete's and he'd call her if I ever showed my face in there again. We went to Pizza Palace instead. Every kid I know has had a birthday party there. They have a bunch of cool old pinball machines and the soda machines are out front, self-serve style.

My mom doesn't let me drink soda at home, and I only get some at the restaurant if I earn it. I don't get soda unless I do a supreme-o job. I'm talking about the kind of help that makes your hands smell worse than your feet. And then I still have to use a small glass.

I sucked down soda and tried to talk about other stuff

besides fountain foam. I told him about the farting door, but Hector has been hearing it fart for ages. He pointed it out to his grandma once, but that just got him a character card. We reminisced about the pizza-eating contest we had at Finn Romo's birthday party. It reminded me of the new girl. I kind of wanted to tell Hector about her, but I didn't.

When we were walking back to the apartment I thought about the new girl and how it would suck to have a birthday at a new school. Then I thought about how it didn't necessarily have to. I told Hector there was something I had to take care of and left. Hector went inside and I headed down the block to Oliver's with an idea.

My Plan

Oliver looked confused when he answered the door.

"I have the next prank. We're having a party," I said.

He walked out into the hall and closed the door behind him.

"What are you talking about? That's not even a prank."

"It could be. It's a surprise party—for everybody!"

"That's still not really a prank," Oliver said. I told him about the new girl transferring to Fountain Point.

"We could throw her a party. She totally won't expect it. It will freak her out!"

Oliver still wasn't sure, but he called Frank and Bean (ha! I just got that) to come over and talk about it. When they got to the apartment we went into Oliver's bedroom and closed the door, just to be safe. Oliver's guitar lay on his bed, and he made a big deal out of putting it back in its case. I think he really wanted us to notice that he had a guitar. It *was* pretty cool. Maybe if the pickle club didn't work out, we could start a band. I don't know how to play any instruments, so I would need to be the singer.

Frank turned on the stereo and held a finger up to his lips. We stood in a huddle, whispering.

"I have an appointment in half an hour," Bean said.

"Video?" Frank asked, and Bean nodded. "You have an appointment with a cat?"

"Yep. His name is Catboy and he's twenty-two pounds! He belongs to a girl in my photography class and he's going to battle Spiderman here." She pulled an action figure out of her pocket with teeth marks on his bicep. "Make it snappy, Ben."

I told them my plan. It was kind of simple, so Bean didn't have time to get impatient.

"So, there was a girl in the office who wouldn't talk to you, and you want to throw her a party?" Frank shrugged. "Why? What's funny about that?"

"Because she won't expect it," I said. "And we could party."

"There's got to be more to it," Frank said.

"Like what?"

"I could make cupcakes," Oliver said. "I can make German chocolate cake. From scratch." He paused for effect, but we just looked at him. I remembered that Oliver had brought chocolate-covered cherry cupcakes that he made to school for the holiday party, and they were pretty delicious. I ate two. All right, three.

"What's German about it?" Bean said.

"I don't know. It's like regular chocolate cake, but better," Oliver said. "I put pecans and coconut in the frosting, so it's full of delicious little lumps. They're chewy. It's awesome."

"Maybe we should figure out what we're doing. This sounds fun, but I'm not sure it's a prank," Frank said.

"Well, I think pranks should be fun. I mean, not mean. Or gross," I said. I'd been giving it some thought.

"Yeah, okay," Oliver said. "I think whatever we do should be funny. Or fun, at least."

"What are you guys saying, we can't permanently scar anybody? I'm out," Bean said, but she didn't go anywhere. She poked Oliver in the forehead. "We've all got to keep it secret. And never rat each other out. Ever." She sent a stink eye around the circle.

"Absolutely," Frank said. "Protect your comrades. Some events may involve an element of danger, but you accept the risks by being a pickle maker."

"What if we each had to set up our own prank? Something that we alone could get busted for," Bean said.

"I like it. Insurance," Frank said.

"Or, um, incentive if anyone is tempted to blab. Oliver," I said.

"I told you guys already, I'm not going to tell. Or brag. Or anything!" he said and held up his hands.

"Then you should be the first to get initiated," I said. "You know, just in case." Oliver rolled his eyes, but he agreed.

"Fine. I'll think of something."

Nobody added anything else, so we all shook on it. "So, by the code, the cupcakes are good but there should be something else," Frank said. "What about the Fountain Point party policy?"

"Fountain Point has a party policy?" Oliver said.

"Don't they?" Frank said. "I thought I might have seen a carefully worded memo stating that all students in the Fountain Point fold should celebrate birthdays with appropriate festivities."

"Yeah, right!" Oliver said. "Principal Lebonsky would never allow something like that."

"Wouldn't she? I think with an appropriately worded notice, an overworked teacher might accept that there *is* a new Fountain Point Birthday Party Policy from our high-handed leader," Frank said.

"I like this," I said. "A lot! But who's going to write the memo?"

"Allow me," Frank said. "We can leave the new policy for Ms. Ruiz to find on her desk when she arrives to class. It will be a direct order from the chief."

"I could get some streamers and stuff from the store," Bean said.

"We'll have to get up extra early to set it all up before school," I said. Frank groaned.

"That won't work. How would we get in? The door will be locked," Oliver said. It was also supposed to rain all weekend, so the windows probably wouldn't be open like last time.

"If I can ensure that you have access to the classroom, can I skip the getting up early part?" Frank said. He asked to borrow Oliver's computer and checked the calendar on the school website. There was a P.T.A. meeting in an hour, so the front doors of the school would be unlocked. Frank said he had to check something out and left. Ten minutes later he came back out of breath and looking smug.

"We're in. Agent Fix-it took care of everything. See you at the party."

"What did you do?" Oliver looked at him suspiciously. "It's not cool if you broke something."

Frank didn't say anything. He just put his finger against his lips in a shushing motion, bowed, and backed out of the room. He really took the whole covert agent thing to heart.

Bean, Oliver, and I agreed to meet at the school at seven on Monday morning. Bean wanted to synchronize our watches, but I didn't think we needed that kind of precision, and Oliver doesn't even own one. Bean would bring some party stuff, and Oliver would bring the cupcakes. I'd grab some chips and stuff from the restaurant. Bean's half hour was up, so she left.

"Wanna check out the new *Mutant Feed* game?" Oliver asked. I did. My dad won't let me play it at home because some of the aliens explode when you punch them. Ten minutes, two levels, and fourteen exploded aliens later it was time to go home.

"Monday's gonna rock. Even if the new girl doesn't like it, it will still be fun," I said, but I hoped she would.

Sienna's Surprise

Oliver and I carried four beer boxes full of chips, grapes, and three-dozen chocolate chip cupcakes with vanilla frosting and sprinkles to school on Monday morning. I snagged the boxes from the restaurant to be covert and disguise the party supplies. You couldn't tell what we had inside the boxes at all. I couldn't wait to tell Frank about my smooth undercover moves, until we got to the steps of the school and I realized that a couple of kids carrying boxes of beer into the school looked way more suspicious than cupcakes.

Bean sat cross-legged in the hall in her red "Stand Back" overalls waiting for us. She had a couple of big blue plastic bags that said Lee's Costume & Party in swirly letters on the side and the official party policy notice from Frank. It said student birthdays were "occasions to celebrate developing maturity" and that teachers should allow enough time before class to enjoy the "celebratory atmosphere provided by a carefully selected party-planning committee." It was signed by Principal Lebonsky at the bottom, but I think the smiley face over the first *i* was pushing our luck. Frank added a P.S. that the new policy was not open to discussion, which was a nice touch. Less chance that Ms. Ruiz would call the office.

"Is the door locked?" I whispered.

"I don't know, I didn't try it," Bean whispered back.

"What do we tell Ms. Ruiz, if she's in there?"

"She won't be in there," Bean said.

"You don't know."

Bean reached for the door. I noticed some fresh scratches on her arm that were probably courtesy of Catboy.

"Eager beavers, early birds!" Pat the secretary's voice echoed through the empty hall and all three of us spun around like disco dancers at a club called Panic. Cold sweat popped out of my forehead. I could not have been more freaked out if she had a ski mask and said it was a stickup.

She stood smiling behind us holding a purple purse and a box of file folders. "Good morning, you three! Whatcha got there?" She nodded toward the boxes Oliver and I still held. Bean had Principal Lebonsky's "memo" behind her back.

"Um, costumes? We're doing a skit based on a Greek myth," Oliver said. I held back a groan. What if she asked to see the costumes? He could have just said decorations and she probably wouldn't have asked any more questions. I wondered if she could see my heart beating.

"Ben is the kraken," Bean said. "I'm Aphrodite. And Oliver is, um, a hippocampus."

"Hippo what?" Oliver said, and Bean elbowed him.

"I don't think I know that one," Pat said. "Anyway, it's nice to see students eager to entertain their classmates."

"That we are," Oliver said. "We even made a little dance number." Pat's eyebrows went up. *Too much*, I thought. *He better have some* Hello, Dolly! *dance ready because I am a boy without rhythm.*

"I'll let you get to it. Have fun, kiddos!" She continued down the hall to the office. I leaned my head on the door and took a deep breath. I balanced the boxes on my knee and pulled on the door handle. It opened without any resistance. The classroom was dark and empty. Bean opened and closed the door a couple more times and bent over to inspect the doorknob.

"Clever Agent Fix-it," she said. Frank had taped the latch down with clear packing tape. The door closed and looked normal, but even with the lock button pushed in the latch was stuck in the door and all you had to do was pull. He was good.

We peeled the tape off and ducked into the classroom, locking the door behind us. I closed the blinds over the windows, so nobody outside could see what we were doing.

Bean cleared off some books in the middle of Ms. Ruiz's desk and propped the memo up where she would see it first thing. I hoped they'd never dust it for fingerprints.

"Check it out," Bean said, and took the party loot out of the bags.

"Huh," Oliver said.

"What's wrong?" Bean asked.

"I didn't know they made brown streamers," Oliver said.

"They make all colors. The brown was on sale."

"No kidding," he said. Bean stopped taking things out of the bags and crossed her arms.

"Did you actually pay for these?" he asked.

"No, I don't buy things from our own store. But I don't want to steal the best stuff. They can sell it. And they'd notice," Bean said.

"What else do you have?"

"There are some green streamers, too. And plates and napkins and stuff," she said.

"Fine, where are the balloons?"

"In the bag."

"We have to blow them up? Why didn't you do it with the machine?"

"Oh, I don't know. I thought a bunch of balloons might be a little conspicuous. Besides, the store doesn't open until nine, and the tank is noisy."

"All right, I'm sorry," Oliver said. "Wait—the plates say

Year of the Pig! We can't use these. She'll think we're calling her a pig!" I grabbed a pack of balloons and started blowing.

"They're from Chinese New Year, goober. I had to get stuff from the clearance bins. I can't just grab *anything*." Oliver complained again until Bean pushed him away. "Don't use the plates then. Cupcakes don't need plates anyway."

Oliver shook his head and grabbed streamers and tape. He wound two streamers together and climbed over desks to hang them every which way. Bean wrote "HAPPY BIRTHDAY, SIENNA!" in big puffy letters on the whiteboard. I threw some Class of 2011 confetti over the desks and set the cupcakes out on a half-squished cardboard tray shaped like a pink Easter bunny. Then I blew up balloons until I made myself dizzy. Bean and Oliver took over. We finished with time to spare.

"It might look better if we aren't the first ones here," Oliver said. We locked the door behind us and took the empty boxes and pig plates out to the recycling bin. Bean walked one way, and we walked another. We looped around back to our block so we could walk to school all over again, looking like we did not expect to find a classroom decorated like a party store threw up in it.

Frank was standing there with most of the other kids waiting for Ms. Ruiz to open the door by the time we got back. He looked cool. Bean touched her nose and pulled on her earlobe, and Frank nodded. If those guys were going to use secret hand signals, they should teach us, too. I glanced over at Oliver. He had a weird look on his face like he felt happy and confused all at once, even though nothing was really happening. I think he was trying to look innocent, but if you ask me, it made him look suspicious. I went to stand by Hector.

"Who's that?" he nodded down the hallway. Sienna stood back away from the others against the lockers. She held on to her backpack like someone would try to yank it off. It looked new. Her clothes looked new, too.

"Dunno, a new girl, I guess," I said. "She's kind of pretty, don't you think?" Hector looked like I'd suggested he use his skateboard for firewood.

Ms. Ruiz moseyed over with her coat on and car keys still in her hand.

"I'm not in the mood for a Monday," she announced to anybody close enough to hear, and opened the door.

The classroom looked kind of fantastic. Even better than it had looked with the balls. Oliver had twisted up the brown and green streamers and attached them all to the fluorescent lights that hung down the middle of the ceiling. It looked like a giant octopus. Red and silver balloons were everywhere, and applause broke out when the class spotted the tray of cupcakes and other snacks. Ms. Ruiz set her purse down on her desk and picked up the memo. She didn't look freaked out, just kind of dazed. Leo Saylor stuffed a cupcake in his mouth and read the whiteboard. "Who's Sienna?" Sprinkles sprayed out of his mouth and onto my shirt.

Sienna was the girl standing by the door, still holding her backpack straps. She didn't raise her hand or anything, but she smiled just a little bit. It wasn't an "I just found $100!" smile, but it was there.

About half of the kids asked who Sienna was before chowing down on cupcakes, and half waited until afterward. Ms. Ruiz seemed confused by the whole thing, but she said okay when someone asked if they could turn some music on. She talked to Sienna for a couple of minutes, and then she yelled over the music for everyone to welcome our new classmate. Everybody yelled hi and toasted her with cupcakes. Some kids yelled thanks. Sienna sat down at a desk and Bean brought her a cupcake. I wished I had thought to bring sodas or at least juice boxes. Some of the other girls started talking to her, too, and asking if she'd made the cupcakes. I watched her shake her head no, but she didn't elaborate. She just smiled and picked the crumbs and sprinkles off of her cupcake paper. Oliver looked proud—like he might tell the class that *he* made the cupcakes. He was smiling really big and standing up straight enough to puff his chest out. I shook my head when I caught his eye and his shoulders slumped, but he nodded.

After the cupcakes, everyone ate the chips and grapes. Even those were gone in less than five minutes. Ms. Ruiz turned the music off after only two songs and said we needed to start class, but we could leave the decorations up. I think she just didn't want the hassle of having to take them down. She read the *Ramayana* to calm us down, but it didn't really work since it's full of fighting monkeys and stuff. Frank threw me a note folded into a star.

They don't know it was us. They think Principal Lebonsky threw the new girl a party!

I shrugged. I felt happy that it worked and we didn't get caught. Ms. Ruiz never even called the office. It felt like a freebie. Frank shook his head and scribbled a new note.

We need people to know it's us.

We need to have a name so we can take the credit.

Like Zorro!

Frank was right again.

Reward

From: Agent Fix-it
To: Oliver Swanson
Cc: Agent Queso; Agent Super
Subject: Initiation
Let me show you how it's done. —AF

I knew what Frank's message was about as soon as I got to school. Green flyers hung everywhere. On the front doors, through the halls, on the bulletin boards. There were even a couple on the office door. He'd beaten Oliver to the punch.

MISSING!

Sense of humor.

If found, please return to the office ASAP.

Reward!

The flyers were up for the first two classes until somebody with no sense of humor took them down. Is that irony? I don't know, but check it out: I heard a kid telling his dad about it that night at Lupe's. I needed to come up with something really good so I could be a member of my own club.

20

Suspects

"Ms. Ruiz said that the new girl got a party because of a new school rule, but none of my other teachers know anything about it. I asked," Maggie said. "Why would anybody throw a party for a kid they hadn't met yet?"

"I don't know," I said. It wasn't a whole lie.

"Wait a minute . . ." She sat there with her mouth open, just squinting at the ceiling. "Do you think it was the same people who filled the class with balls? Why would somebody keep sneaking into our classroom?" Maggie chewed her thumbnail.

"I don't know," I said.

Kids were talking about what would happen next. The leading theory going around was that the balls and the party were from someone inside our homeroom class. Their powers of deduction amazed me. And made me want to throw up a little bit. Leo Saylor wrote everyone's name on a long list labeled "Suspects." We were pretty much all on it. Except Leo. He didn't put his own name down. He said he didn't have time to do goofy stuff like that, and everybody believed him. My name was near the top. Frank, Bean, and Oliver were on there, too. The pressure was on.

Banana Bread Bribery

"Good morning, students!" Pat's voice came over the P.A. and interrupted Ms. Ruiz's talk about lake monsters and dragons. "Imagine my surprise this morning when the heater came on in the office and I was showered with confetti. Confetti, I tell you! Some clever trickster put a great deal of confetti in our office vents. I enjoyed the rain, but I'm afraid Principal Lebonsky won't have the same, ah, appreciation. It looks like her office got the worst of it." There was mumbling and the intercom clicked off. Ms. Ruiz took a breath to get back into her mythological creature talk. The P.A. clicked back on. "Pat here, again. If anybody wants to volunteer to help Rick and me clean up the confetti before Principal Lebonsky gets back from a school district meeting, there will be some banana bread in it for you. Thank you."

Oliver stopped Bean and me on the way out of class.

"Mission accomplished. Consider me an official, initiated pickle maker," he said. Bean high-fived him.

"Where'd you get the confetti?" she said.

"I bought it at Party Plus. I didn't want it to get traced back to Lee's."

"They can't trace confetti! Way to take food out of my mouth, bro," she said. Oliver looked like he might apologize, so I talked before he could.

"Nice work. How'd you think to put it in the vents?"

"I used to hide stuff in the heater vent at my last foster house. There was another kid there that swiped stuff," he said.

"Pretty clever, Oliver," I said.

"We'll call you Clevoliver." Bean tapped him on top of the head with her pencil like she was knighting him. I don't call him that, but she does. A lot.

A Club with No Name

"Frank suggests that our group needs a name, and I think so, too," I said on Thursday at the beginning of our second pickle meeting. Everybody nodded.

"We could leave a sign out for everyone to see when we pull off a prank. We *should* take credit," Oliver said. Bean agreed. The League of Pickle Makers would obviously blow our cover, so we needed another name, too.

"Something with cool initials like the C.I.A.," Frank said.

"G.O.O.F.," Oliver said.

"What does it stand for?" I asked.

"Um . . . Great . . . Order . . . Of . . . um . . . Friends," Oliver mumbled.

"That . . . doesn't . . . sound . . . so . . . great," Bean said.

"How about Awesome Secret Society?" Oliver said. I thought he might be onto something for about eleven seconds until I figured it out. Bean hit him in the back of the head.

"How about the Secret Agency of Pranksters?" I said. It made us sound like covert, funny, super spies.

"You want to be a S.A.P.?" Frank asked. I did not.

Bean suggested we just think of words that would match the acronym D.U.M.B. After many, many bad ideas, we finally came up with a name that everyone agreed wasn't too bad—the Prank and Trick Association. The name itself was only so-so, but if we used the initials our signs could say:

"Today's entertainment brought to you compliments of the P.T.A. Thank you."

It was kind of true, since the P.T.A. gave us money to start the club. Bean would print the cards out with some fancy cursive font on thick paper that they used for wedding invitations at the store.

"We could make a cool sign for the Pioneer Fair, too," Oliver said. "But, you know, for the League of Pickle Makers. Not the P.T.A."

"I guess so," I said. "As long as it's not the same color paper or writing as the P.T.A. signs."

"No doubt. That would be bad," Bean said. "The store has a roll of bright green paper that we can use to make a banner for the Pioneer Fair."

"I don't know. You two haven't done your initiation yet. Since you're not full members, I'm not sure that you'll get a vote," Oliver said. He made air quotes when he said "full members."

"Oh, Clevoliver. I'm not sure you'll get to bend your fingers into cute little quotation marks anymore if you keep talking to us like that," Bean said. "When I do my prank, you're gonna know. It's going to be legendary." I thought it might be better to do mine before Bean did hers. I just hadn't thought of anything yet.

"Cool it, guys. Listen. Let's have a website," Frank said. He said he'd made tons of websites before. But, he wouldn't tell us what they were—other than Bean's Cat vs. Dude. We moved the meeting to the library to use the computers. The chess club was already in there, so we had to keep our voices down. We crowded around the computer farthest from the other kids. Frank showed us a site where you could pick a domain name. We found that most sites that have P.T.A. in the name were taken. They were probably all teacher and parent magnets anyway.

"I'm glad that we're doing this," Bean said. She elbowed me kind of hard, but when I looked up she smiled. I thought she meant making a website, but then I realized she meant the club. I wanted to tell her that I thought she was cool, that I'd been wrong about her before, but I couldn't think of a way to do it that didn't sound bad.

“Yeah,” I said.

“Pickles forever!” Oliver said. I think he meant “I’m-happy-we’re-friends-too-and-this-is-fun,” but Frank thought it was a website suggestion. He checked, and www.picklesforever.com wasn’t taken.

“Wait a minute. We can’t put prank stuff on there. People will know the pickle club is doing it,” I whispered.

“We can make it *appear* to be an ode to the pickle, but I’ll encrypt a password to see the good stuff,” Frank said.

“What’s the good stuff?” Oliver said.

Silence.

“Duh, pranks!” Bean shook her head. “How about if we post videos?”

“Too risky. Someone might identify us. Reports,” Frank said.

"What kind of reports? Like a book report?"

"No. Incident reports. Like the cops do. Pranks, Instructions. Kids from all over could come and learn how to do pranks at *their* schools if we tell them the password. We could still keep some stuff hidden. The P.T.A. could be HUGE," Frank said.

"We could go viral," Bean said.

"Like a computer virus?" I asked. I wasn't allowed to download stuff without checking it for viruses. Maybe it was because of Bean.

"Like a flu virus," Bean said. I ignored her. "Catch up, Ben. Not like a computer virus. Like something that spreads around the Internet so that people all over see it. Like a kitten video." Points for not mentioning her own website. She hardly ever had kittens in the videos. Not that I check. I have at least five kitten videos bookmarked, from other websites, but I wasn't going to tell them that. I just nodded.

"I'll get started on this and have something for you guys to see next week," Frank said. He shooed us out of the library, and we went to check on the pickles we had made in the lab. We'd take them to the Pioneer Fair, everybody would be impressed that kids made pickles, and we'd get a cash prize. It was perfect.

Except one thing: When we got to the lab, the pickles were gone.

Check-In

"Why don't you tell me what's been happening," Ms. Ruiz said. She had asked me to stay after school Friday for another League of Pickle Makers check-in meeting.

"What do you mean?" I said.

"Well, how are things going for the Pioneer Fair?"

"Oh, right," I said. "Fine, I guess."

"What have you decided to prepare à la the pioneers?"

"Pickles," I said.

"Well, of course, Ben! I assumed you'd be preparing pickles. You *are* a pickle maker. Which variety of pickle do you plan on preparing?" Ms. Ruiz smiled at me. I wanted to tell her that she talked like a tongue twister, but I didn't.

"Well, we made some . . . basic . . . pickles, and left them in the lab to . . . sit. But, somebody took them."

"What do you mean?"

"I went to check on them yesterday, and they were gone. The jar and everything," I said. Ms. Ruiz nodded and looked like she thought that it was totally reasonable that there would be a pickle thief at the school.

"Where were the pickles?" she asked.

"Just up on the counter in the laboratory," I said. Ms. Ruiz nodded again.

"Rick probably thought they were left over from a science experiment. I'll arrange for a cupboard to be set aside *exclusively* for the League of Pickle Makers." Ms. Ruiz made a note on a notepad covered in coffee stain rings. I thanked her and got up to leave. There just isn't that much pickle business to discuss.

"Ben, you had better gather your picklers together to prepare for the Pioneer Fair. It's just a few weeks away," she said. "Most of the better pickling recipes take that long to cure."

"We'll get started on something," I said.

"Excellent. I've been making arrangements with the other club advisors. The baking club will definitely be participating, and some of the others. The art club made arrangements for a leather-punching demonstration." I pictured people fighting motorcycle jackets, but I felt pretty sure it was something else.

"That's great," I said, and got up from my chair.

"One more thing, Ben," Ms. Ruiz said. "Do you know

anything about the pranks that have been going on around school?"

"Why would I know anything about the pranks?" I said. My mouth felt like it was full of cotton balls. Dirty, lying cotton balls. My eye twitched.

"Principal Lebonsky has a theory that what has been happening would take more than one student, so one of the groups at school may be responsible," Ms. Ruiz said.

"Oh."

"I told her that I didn't think it was likely, but she said that the clubs have school access after classes. She's asked the faculty advisors to question all club leaders."

"Other kids could come into the school when it's open for extracurricular enrichment," I said.

"Exactly!" Ms. Ruiz said. "I have you pickle makers and girls' basketball. I told her that I'm sure that none of my students would do anything to jeopardize themselves. You've got enough on your plate with the Pioneer Fair; no time for mischief!" She laughed and shook her head.

I went straight home after the meeting and emailed the club to tell them what Ms. Ruiz said about the fair and the pranks. Well, I emailed their agent accounts. Bean had chosen to go by Agent Super, and Oliver was Agent 008. I sent the message in Italian. I told them that we needed to make a new plan for pickles for the fair, but nobody responded. I forwarded a couple of pickle recipes.

All these guys had to do was say whether the recipes looked good or not. I checked my email four more times, but they'd ignored the recipes. I slammed the computer closed and turned on the TV.

Trick #3

After I checked my email a couple more times, I caught the second half of *Escape from Zombie High.* It wasn't as funny as I hoped, but the final scene when the star football player got cornered in the gym by the mob of angry zombie cheerleaders gave me an idea for my initiation. The gym filled with fog before the attack, and I thought about how cool and creepy it would be to have our gym floor like that, full of swirling, misty clouds. Like zombie cheerleaders were going to grab you when you tried to climb the rope. That's what one of the guys in the movie did. He tried to climb the rope but he only got about five feet before the zombie girls pulled him down. I don't know what he was thinking. Nobody can climb those ropes very fast, and it's just hanging from a hook on the ceiling. It's not like he could escape. Still, it gave me an idea.

"I know what I want to do for my solo prank, but I need a little help," I said. The pickle makers were eating lunch together in the quietest corner of the cafeteria.

"Help? No help. *Solo* mission," Frank said. I leaned across the table.

"I've already proven that I can do it alone, haven't I? I'm pretty sure I could just count the balls as my initiation. But, I'll be a good sport and just say that was a freebie."

"Noted," Frank said. "What do you have in mind?"

"Let's fog up the gym. All of the classes go, so it wouldn't just be Ms. Ruiz's class again. It would be like a zombie movie."

"Spooky, I like it. But how?" Bean said.

"Well, do you guys sell fog machines in the store?"

"Yeah, but they're, like, fifty dollars. We can't borrow one either because the boxes are all shrink-wrapped. How much club money do we have left?" I checked the envelope in my backpack.

"Twenty-one bucks. And thirty-eight cents," I said. "It's not enough."

"Maybe not for a fog machine, but there's always dry ice," Frank said. Oliver didn't know what it was, so Frank explained how dry ice was really frozen carbon dioxide that makes misty fog when you put it in water. Perfect. I'd seen a sign for dry ice blocks at the bodega on the corner. Oliver had to go to a rehearsal for *Hello, Dolly!*, so we made plans to meet there before school the next day, and Bean would bring some disposable popcorn bowls from Lee's to hold the water.

Operation Zombie Gym was a go.

The Fog

I overslept, so the others were already waiting in front of the bodega when I ran up. Oliver pointed to a sign on the door that said only one kid was allowed in the store at a time. It was one of *those* places. We wanted to buy the dry ice as a group, so we walked three blocks to Farley's Grocery. They sell dry ice, too. They keep it by the front doors in a cooler.

Did you know that touching dry ice without gloves burns your hands? I did not. I found out the hard way when I reached into the cooler to throw a couple blocks into our cart. It felt crazy cold, and then started burning a split second later. Oliver said I squeaked, but I think I made more of a manly sound. Like a grunt. Whatever it was, it hurt, and the sound I made was loud enough that the cashier came to see what we were doing.

The cashier, whose name tag said we should call him Eddie, told me it would have been a lot worse if the blocks weren't wrapped in plastic, and what kind of numbskull was I anyway to not use gloves. Then he pulled a pair on a chain from the back of the freezer. I don't know why I didn't think to look behind the freezer for something I didn't know I needed. Eddie put the gloves on, but then shut the freezer door and put his hands on his hips.

"What do you kids want dry ice for anyway?"

"For a school project," I said.

"It's not a toy."

"We know that."

"I'm not sure if we should even sell this to kids. Look what already happened." He nodded toward me, with my stinging fingers in my mouth.

"Is there an age limit?" Oliver said. Eddie's eyes flared a little bit, like we'd challenged him to a duel. He inspected the freezer all over and read all of the fine print on the sticker on the door. There were teeny tiny faded letters that said you should wear gloves when handling dry ice, but nothing about an age limit. Eddie checked the sides and the back where the glove chain was attached. He shook his head.

"I'm sorry, but I just don't think you guys need this stuff," Eddie said. Frank cleared his throat.

"My parents, the biology PROFESSOR and the LAWYER, would be very curious to know why we were not able to obtain the solidified carbon dioxide required for the important experiments in the LABORATORY to expand our scientific EDUCATION," Frank said.

Eddie stared at Frank until Oliver stepped forward.

"This unnecessary delay may cause us to be tardy for school, sir. Surely you do not wish to encroach on our rights to a well-rounded education? I believe our principal would be very interested in hearing your explanation for this outrage. An outrage, I say!" Oliver yelled, his right arm raised and pointing toward Farley's water-stained ceiling.

I thought he'd gone too far. Maybe Eddie knew Principal Lebonsky, and next time she stopped in to buy vegetables for Hector he would tell her about the blabbermouth kids trying to buy dry ice for who knows what. Maybe he'd even give her our descriptions. I got so caught up in picturing the four of us in a lineup being ID'd by Eddie that I didn't notice when he started loading blocks into a box.

"How much do you kids want, anyway?" Eddie said. Bean elbowed me.

"Uh, twenty-one dollars worth." Eddie sighed, but he packed four blocks into an empty hot dog box. Each one was about the size of half a shoe box. Frank saw me looking at the blocks and read my mind.

"Don't worry. Just wait until we add water."

We bought a pack of grape bubble gum with the change from the ice and took off to school. We walked quickly to get back and put the ice in the gym before Coach Capell got done running laps around the track. I've seen that guy out there in a snowstorm, and during heat waves, too. He's a little nutty.

"Are your parents really a lawyer and a biology professor?" I asked Frank. I thought they'd be F.B.I. agents, or professional computer hackers.

"They run a day care," he said.

We headed into the gym with the box of dry ice and four bowls. "If you just leave them out here, Coach Capell will see and throw them away before class even starts," Frank said.

"Where should we put them then?" I said.

"I don't know," Bean said. "Somewhere more private? Let's think . . . Maybe with an arm pit aroma and some leaky taps?"

"Oh, the locker room? Okay. I'll take two into the boys'—do you want to put the other two in the girls'?" Bean shook her head before I even finished talking.

"I would . . . but this isn't *my* prank. You've got to take the risk. Seems like you should handle fog placement personally." Bean held a bowl out to me.

"I can't go in the girls' locker room! C'mon, Bean. Please? We could do this one together. You haven't done your initiation yet."

"It's just not going to happen, Diaz," Bean said. "I'm cooking up something else to prove *I'm* worthy." She handed me the bowl. I couldn't ask the other guys to do it for me. I thought about calling off the prank. Bean bounced around on her feet, soaking up all of my discomfort like she was a sponge.

"Fine, there's probably nobody in there anyway."

"Unless the cheerleaders are here. Practicing early," Oliver said. "I'm sure they won't mind seeing you in their locker room. That's not creepy at all."

I had to do it. I put my sweatshirt over my hands before I took the blocks out of the box and put them into the bowls. I carried two to the boys' locker room. I stood on the bench to slide the bowls on top of the lockers so people wouldn't touch them by accident. Frank grabbed his water bottle out of his locker, and I poured some into each bowl, but they were too high to see what was happening. When I got down, I couldn't see the bowls at all, but a couple of thin wisps of mist were falling down the lockers.

I stood at the doorway to the girls' locker room and listened. I didn't hear anyone inside, but my hyperventilating might have muffled any voices.

I tried to stand up straight and look confident. If somebody was there, maybe they'd think I was on some sort of official business. I went inside.

It didn't smell as bad as the boys' locker room, but otherwise it was pretty much the same, and I was able to fill the bowls up with water and put them on top of the lockers. I was out in less than three minutes. The gym was still deserted, besides the P.T.A.

Soon, there would be clouds of mystery!

"Will it drift out here into the gym like there's an impending zombie attack?"

"Have patience, Ben. Remember the bubbles," Bean said, and patted me on the back. "Or you can stick your hands in there and swish it around." They laughed. I didn't. Voices echoed in the gym lobby. The closest place to hide was the boys' locker room, so we ran in there. Oliver ducked around the corner into the shower room, but there wasn't anywhere to hide there. Frank folded himself into his locker and closed the door without a sound. Bean did the same thing with another locker a few doors down.

"Dude, I left it in my locker. It will just take a minute!" somebody whined, and the locker-room door creaked open. I boosted myself up from the bench to lay flat on top of the lockers by the bowl. It was starting to fog up a little bit and make hissing, gurgly sounds.

Two tall boys came in. Eighth graders. I recognized them from the basketball team. The shorter one once gave me and Finn Romo directions to the janitor's closet when we asked him how to get to the cafeteria. I peeked over the edge of the lockers to see which way they'd gone, and caught a glimpse of the tops of their heads. The shorter one had dandruff. I scooted back as slowly as I could, but the lockers creaked from the shifting weight.

"Shhh. Did you hear that?" the big one said. I held my

breath. I heard one of them grab a locker door and jerk it open. There was a scream, and I think it was the tall guy. "What are you doing in my locker?" he said. I snuck another look over the edge. He held Bean up by the front of her overalls. She just scowled at him. "You are so dead, shorty." We were busted. We were busted. We were busted.

"Oh, yeah? What are you going to do to me, pudding brain?" Bean said. We were busted.

"I'm going to tell Mom, that's what. You aren't allowed to mess with my stuff! How long have you been waiting in there to scare me?"

"All morning, big guy." Bean smiled.

"Well, you're going to be in trouble tonight. You're not supposed to be in the boys' locker room, weirdo," he said. "And you didn't scare me." He put her down and tried to pinch her nose, but Bean was too fast for him. She tried to smack him on his way out of the locker room, but she only caught a little bit of his shoulder. Their voices got farther away, but I didn't slide down from the lockers until I heard the gym door slam. Frank climbed out of the other locker.

"You have a brother?"

"I have brothers."

"Did you know that was his locker?"

"Nope."

We headed to history class and tried to look calm until gym class started an hour later.

I have never, ever been so excited to start gym class, not even when we got to have a water balloon fight. Oliver and I hung back a little bit so we wouldn't be the first ones into the locker room and we could check out everyone's reactions. I heard laughter from the locker room while we were still crossing the gym.

Two blocks of dry ice in each locker room equals a puny four-and-a-half-foot pool of fog. It just sat there like a chunk of sick cloud, no bigger than a table at the restaurant. It didn't even swirl, and as soon as Leo Saylor kicked his leg through the mist, it was pretty much gone. I hoped the girls' locker room had a better effect, but the snickering coming through the vent told me it was probably about the same. At least the class laughed, but it felt more like an "at us" laugh than a "with us" laugh. Somebody said it was funky locker gas and we all started pointing fingers. Hector pointed at me and I pointed at Oliver. I hoped that Frank and Bean had forgotten the cards, but there they were taped to the mirror over the sinks.

This creepy atmosphere brought to you compliments of the P.T.A. Thank you.

"The only thing creepy is the smell from the showers," Finn said. No zombie would have shown his green face at our wimpy fog fest.

The most dramatic reaction came from Coach Capell. Somebody told him about the mystery mist, and he blew his whistle and yelled, "Evacuate the area! This is not a drill!" He talked about harmful gases and made us run laps outside while Rick "took care of the matter."

"Operation Zombie Gym sucked," Frank said when he ran past. Like I didn't know.

Principal Lebonsky made an announcement during science class. She said, "Whomever deposited the dry ice in the locker rooms created a hazard for fellow students and violated school policy by posting unapproved signage on the mirrors. I am out of patience with the recent mischief, and I vow that there will be appropriate consequences for all responsible parties."

The rest of the day didn't get any better. Mr. Reynolds gave us a pop quiz on the parts of a frog, and I got a C on my essay about Hermes. When I got home, all I wanted to do was veg out in front of the TV. I dug into my backpack for the last piece of gum we'd bought at Farley's and found one of the P.T.A. cards. Frank hadn't given me any yet, so I knew I didn't put it in there.

My heart punched my throat. Why would someone give it to me? Did Coach Capell know we did it? I looked at the card again. A little bit of tape still stuck to the top, so I knew it came from the mirror in the locker room. I turned it over.

I know it was you.
The party 2.
I want in.
—Sienna

Emergency Democracy

I did the only thing I could think of. I called an emergency pickle maker meeting. It had started to rain, but it didn't matter. I grabbed my hoodie and ran out of the building.

The other three were already standing in front of the school under Bean's big black-and-white-checkered umbrella. Oliver was wearing a tuxedo with a yellow vest.

"Wow, Oliver. Are you going to dress up for all of our meetings?" Frank said. Oliver rolled his eyes.

"I had to leave a dress rehearsal. You know, I'm the lead in *Hello, Dolly!*" he said.

"You're Dolly?"

"No, Frank, I'm not. Why does everybody

keep saying that?" Oliver bowed. "I'm Horace Vandergelder."

"It sounds like the lead is Dolly. It's not called *Hello, Horace!*" Frank said. Oliver sighed, like we couldn't possibly understand the theater.

"It's a very important role," he said.

"Whatever you say. What's this about, Ben?" Frank said. I showed them the note.

"She's going to tell," Bean said.

"I don't know," Oliver said. "She doesn't seem like that kind of kid. It's a new school for her. She probably just wants to make friends."

"We're a secret society, not a welcoming committee," Bean said.

"If we don't let her in, she might tell. If we do, she might not," I said.

We stood there arguing in the rain for a while. Bean really didn't want Sienna to be in the club.

"She should be required to show that she is worthy of our esteemed group," Bean said. "The group is invitation only, and she totally just invited herself."

"That's funny, Bean. You know, since you kind of crashed it yourself," I said.

"Not really. Frank invited me," Bean said. Frank did the more-or-less thing with his hand.

"Let's be democratic about it," Oliver said. I think he just wanted to get back to rehearsal.

"No! It should be like a secret fraternity. One black ball and she can't join," Bean said. I was pretty sure who would try and shut her out, and it wasn't any of the dudes.

"You're not a full member of the P.T.A. yet, Bean. How are those solo prank plans coming along?" She just smirked at me. "All in favor of inviting Sienna to join the club," I said. Three hands went up. My theory was confirmed. Bean looked pretty mellow about it, for a few seconds.

"We have to let Sienna in for cuteness alone," Frank said, and raised his hand to get a high five from Bean. She shoved him into the gutter and stomped off down the street, taking her umbrella with her. Meeting adjourned.

Nobody Expects the Pickle Inquisition

Monday morning I slipped the P.T.A. card into Sienna's locker with a note on the bottom. It said that our next meeting was after school on Thursday in the lab, and she could meet us there. I didn't say who the "us" was, and I didn't sign the note. She'd slipped the card into my backpack, but I wasn't sure how much she knew. Or *thought* she knew.

Sienna waited in silence in the hall outside the laboratory with Frank and Oliver. We went inside when I got there, but Bean was late. I asked Sienna how she liked Fountain Point so far and she just shrugged. She wore a little silver feather on a chain around her neck. I wanted to ask her what made her smell so good, but I didn't. Today she smelled like flowers. And cake. If the roses on top of a birthday cake really smelled like roses, and you combined it with all the frosting and cake goodness, that would be the way Sienna smelled. She wasn't wearing any lip gloss, but her eyelids looked a little glittery.

Bean came into the lab and whacked her backpack down on top of the table.

"You're late," Frank said. She didn't answer, but she sat down and narrowed her eyes at Sienna.

"Why would you want to join our club? If that's what we are," Bean said. Sienna rolled her eyes.

"You guys seem fun, and I haven't really found anyone to hang out with yet."

"I see. Do you like pickles?" Bean took out a furry brown notebook and a pen.

"No," Sienna said. "I like cherry peppers, though." Bean *tsk*ed and wrote something in the notebook.

"Where were you before this? Why'd you move?"

"Colorado," Sienna blinked. "We just did."

"What makes you think that Ben knows anything about the events that have been happening around school?"

"Quit trying to play dumb, all right? I know it was Ben because he was the only one in the office when that secretary said it was my birthday. I didn't tell anyone else," Sienna said. Bean didn't even look up, but she continued to write in her notebook.

"Good deduction," Frank said. "Tell us, what makes you think you're a good candidate for the League of Pickle Makers?"

"The League of what?" Sienna looked around the group. "You're kidding, right? That's your name?" Nobody answered. "I thought you guys were doing the pranks."

"That's one of our names. We're asking the questions, if you don't mind," Frank continued. "You're the new kid, you have that going for you. Nobody will believe that you're in on any inside jobs. What do your parents do?"

"What does that matter?" Sienna said.

"Bean's mom and dad own a party shop where we may obtain our necessary supplies. Ben's parents have a restaurant where the club can meet if the laboratory is ever compromised. These are assets," Frank said. I noticed that he didn't mention the day care. "My question is whether your family could be useful to the operation."

"My mom is a real estate agent."

"And your dad? What does he do?" Bean asked. Sienna stared her down before answering.

"He calls from Denver on Saturdays. Sometimes." She looked at the floor for a minute, and then up at Bean, like she dared her to ask another question.

"Any brothers or sisters?" I said. Just to say something.

"I have a big sister," she said. "She's still in Denver."

"Well, real estate doesn't give us a lot to work with," Frank said. I tried to think of something cool to say, but I came up blank.

"We must have a solemn oath from you that anything that happens in the club is absolutely top secret," Bean said.

"Sure."

"Say it. And raise your right hand," Bean said. Sienna looked at the rest of us, maybe to see if we would say she didn't have to do it. Nobody did, so she raised her right hand.

"I swear to keep everything that happens in the club totally secret," she said.

"Excellent. Can you bring a roll of saran wrap to school tomorrow?" Oliver said.

"For what?" Sienna asked.

"Let's consider it an initiation into the group," he said. Bean nodded.

"Bring it tomorrow. And pick up some vinegar and dill to keep in your locker," Oliver said. "You do that, and maybe you can be a pickle maker."

Sienna looked at us like we were nuts, but she was the one who had asked to be in the club. Then Bean said Sienna had to leave so we could have official club business.

"Whatever, you guys are crazy," she said, and left.

"I don't think she likes us after all," Bean said. She tried to look disappointed, but she didn't try too hard. I didn't say anything, but I hoped Sienna would be back.

28 The Invisible Barrier

Sienna brought the plastic wrap, and following Oliver's very detailed instructions, wrapped the sinks in the front two bathrooms before school the next morning. She stopped short in front of the boys' room door. "Oliver, could you take a peek and make sure it's empty?" Oliver nodded and headed into the bathroom. I wanted to point out the *major prank foul* that nobody checked the girls' locker room for me before I went inside, but Sienna already looked like she might change her mind. And Oliver had already plowed in before she was even done asking. Oliver came out and gave a subtle thumbs-up on his way back to my locker. Sienna ducked in. She was back out in under two minutes. She tried to throw the box away, but Frank grabbed it back out of the can.

"Stellar work, team. Let's go for the bonus round. Faculty

restrooms," Frank said and handed the roll of plastic wrap back to Sienna.

"Whoa, nice!" Bean said, and high-fived Frank.

"No way. You're just trying to get me busted," Sienna said.

"On the contrary, the League of Pickle Makers is all about a challenge," Frank said.

"What if I don't do it?"

"Then you won't be a pickle maker," Bean said. "Simple. As. That."

"Fine," Sienna said. She grabbed the tube and stomped down the hall. She pretended to tie her shoe while Mr. Reynolds walked past and then she ducked into the men's room first. After about a minute, she opened the door and tiptoed into the women's room. She came back out fast, without the plastic wrap. I thought she had chickened out, or bumped into a teacher in there and gotten busted. But she ran back to us and nodded. "Done."

We could see the student and faculty restrooms from my locker, so we all stood around lurking like we were just hanging out.

"I bet you five bucks nobody falls for it," Sienna said.

"You are on, doorknob," Bean said.

Two girls went into the girls' room. We waited. Two minutes later they came out calm and dry. I thought they must have figured it out and taken the plastic off and Bean owed Sienna a fiver. It turns out they just didn't wash their hands after they peed. After that, a whole bunch of kids got splashed in a row. Girls and boys. It made the front of their pants wet in the *worst* possible spot. Kids came out with red faces holding their books down low in front of them. Nobody used the faculty restrooms, and I tried to remember if I'd *ever* seen anyone going in there.

I pretended to look for something in my locker for twenty minutes, and the others pretended to wait patiently while I searched. Maggie Rubio went into the girls' room and came out with dry pants, so she was definitely in the no-wash club. She waved and I tried to wave back in a casual way like I'd just noticed her and definitely not like I'd been gawking at her coming out of the bathroom and was now grossed out. A dry kid would come out, and we'd groan. I'd think it was over, and then more splashed kids! We tried not to laugh, but that just made it worse. We had just given up on any grown-ups using the faculty bathroom when Coach Capell went inside.

"Fine, you're in," Bean whispered. "Set up a secret email account, but *don't* use your real name. Think up a code agent name. Frank is Agent Fix-it, and Oliver is Agent 008. Wait, why are you Agent 008?"

"Because, I am the next Sean Connery," Oliver said. "You know, James Bond. 007? Sean Connery played him in the movies. And Roger Moore, Daniel Craig, and someday, Oliver Swanson." We just stared at him. "It's a great role!"

"Sure, okay. I'll be Agent Snow," Sienna said.

"Why snow?" I asked.

"There's a lot of it in Colorado. I like it." Sienna shrugged. "Maybe we should get out of here now." The rest of us voted to stay. All five of us looked at my math workbook like we were trying to find a missing integer, if looking for a missing integer was hilarious and math was fun! The bathroom door opened and our laughter died down to one last snort from Oliver. Coach Capell came out dry, but he didn't look mad. You know what that means.

Another twenty kids went into the student restrooms. Awesome part: nobody thought to take the plastic off or warn other kids, so it just kept happening until the bell rang and class started. Classic.

A Visitor

"We, uh, need to make some new pickles," I said as soon as I came into the lab for the Thursday pickle maker meeting. "I saw Ms. Ruiz. The fair is coming up *really* soon." I pointed to the Pioneer Fair poster on the wall and pulled *The Joy of Pickling* out of my backpack. I'd looked through it the night before, but I didn't find any speedy recipes. Fish doesn't take that long to pickle, but I knew we couldn't do it after seeing the pickled herring pictures. I brought *The Joy of Pickling* back to school specifically so they could all see the lovely plate of gray lumps.

"The parsley garnish doesn't hide the disgusting, does it?" I said. Frank looked closer.

"What are those yellow flecks on the top?"

"Grated egg yolk," I said.

"No way. I'm not touching that. We're doomed," Oliver said.

"Not necessarily. Couldn't we just buy some pickles and enter those?" Bean suggested.

"I think that's kind of sleazy," Frank said. "C'mon. How hard can it be?"

Someone tapped on the door.

"Who is at the door?" Bean looked at me, like I'd invited Principal Lebonsky to drop by.

"I don't know," I said.

"Do not open it," Frank said, but the person on the other side opened it.

It was Hector. He waved at us and walked in carrying his old, beat-up skateboard.

"Hey, guys," he said.

"Hey, Hector," Bean said, and smiled. "What could you possibly be doing here?"

"I think I'm a pickle maker. I mean, I think I could be. I'd like to be," he said. Maybe he'd figured out what we were doing, like Sienna. Did everybody know what was going on? It was possible that we were not the anonymous prank masters we thought we were. We didn't even leave P.T.A. signs up by the plastic-wrapped sinks. I tried to think of a question I could ask him to find out whether he meant pickle maker or "pickle maker."

"Oh, um, why? You don't even like pickles," I said. Hector looked hurt, like it was an insult.

"They're not so bad. I've been thinking about giving them

another try." He inspected the trucks on his skateboard and scraped some gunk off with his thumbnail.

"What? You're here because you want to make pickles? With us? Really?" Bean asked. Hector looked at me, and then the others, like he wasn't sure anymore, but then he said yes.

"We're working on our pickling contest entry for the Pioneer Fair," Frank said. He gestured to a cutting board and some fluffy green dill leaves Oliver had put on the table. I hadn't even seen him take that stuff out. "How do we know you're not here to scope out the competition?"

"What? That's goofy."

"Did you know about the pickling competition coming up at the Pioneer Fair? Did your granny tell you?" Oliver crossed his arms over his chest.

"No, I just knew Ben did this, and I thought it might be fun. I—"

"—just wanted to check out the competition."

"What? No, I just—"

"We're on to you, Hector. We cannot compromise our secret pickling formula!" Frank yelled. Hector looked at me and started stammering.

"I just want to be—"

"We know what you want. We're going to try and win the contest fair and square, and so should you," Sienna said. Hector stared at her. She shook her head. "If you go now, we won't tell Ms. Ruiz about this."

Hector's face got red. He glared at me, waiting for me to say something. Anything. I wanted to—really, but I just wanted him to leave, too. I tried to apologize with my eyes. He opened his mouth, but then he just shook his head and left. Oliver closed the door behind him.

"That was close," Bean said.

"Yeah," Oliver agreed, and then everybody stared at me. I couldn't look at them. I just waited until my stomach stopped feeling like I ate a bucket of that pickled herring and it was all about to come up.

"So, what are we making for the contest?" I said. I didn't care about making any stupid pickles, but I wanted to stop them from staring at me like that.

Nobody said anything for a while.

"Are you mad at us?" Sienna said.

"No! Why would I be mad?" I said.

"Well, how about because we kicked your best friend out of the lab," Oliver said. "I mean, if you wanted him to join I guess we could talk about it. We could vote, like we did with Sienna." Bean scoffed, but I couldn't tell what Frank was thinking.

"You guys voted to let me in?" Sienna said.

"It's just . . ." I stopped. I didn't want to tell them that I was selfish. That I just wanted the club for myself, and I didn't want to share them. And I didn't want to remind them that he was afraid of his grandma enough to ruin us all. He would be in a big world of hurt if his grandma caught him setting a prank up. "I don't think this would be Hector's kind of thing."

"Which?" Oliver said. "The pickles or the P.T.A.?"

"Either, I guess. But, thanks for the offer. We've been doing everything together for years. It's okay to have a few changes," I said, and they seemed to accept it. I don't know if I did.

We looked through *The Joy of Pickling*, but nothing seemed that exciting. The book was pretty old, so we went to the library to look online. Maybe we could find a newer, cooler pickle recipe.

The computers are right in the middle of the room, so it makes a good lookout. Oliver and Frank talked about pranks we could do in the library while I searched for pickle recipes. There isn't a lot of variety if you stick to cucumbers and stay away from stuff like fish and turkey gizzards. Some people get really crazy with stuffed pickles and pickle ice cream, but I didn't think that was how the pioneers would do it. The pictures made me feel gross again, so Frank took over.

The best we could come up with were bread-and-butter pickles. They weren't really that exciting. They didn't even have any butter. But at least Ms. Ruiz and Principal Lebonsky would think we tried. Some other pickler would be getting the cash prize.

Principal Pickles

"Hey, Hector, wait up!" I found Hector right where I thought I would—in the lunch line reaching for a bowl of mac and cheese. It was the first Friday of the month, and that made it a gooey tradition. He glanced over his shoulder and nodded at me.

"What's up?"

"I just haven't seen you much. How's it going?" He looked annoyed for a second, but then his face relaxed.

"It's Mac Friday. Things are good," Hector said. He grabbed another bowl of mac while the lunch lady's back was turned and seemed miffed that I was watching. "I'll have to make up for it later, anyway. Mac Friday is usually also spinach-salad-for-dinner Friday."

"Sorry." I grabbed a lunch tray and followed Hector. "What about dinner at my house? I don't know what we're having, but there's an eighty percent chance that it's better than that." Hector didn't answer, so I kept talking. "We could watch a movie? Or skate?"

"Yeah, no thanks. I'll just stick with the salad." Hector picked up his tray and walked past me to Leo and Finn's table. I sat down with the pickle makers and tried not to look at Hector's table. Hector caught up with me after lunch on my way out of the cafeteria.

"You could sleep over at my house, if you want to," he said. "My grandma might make something better than spinach salad if you're there." I said yes.

Hector was right. Principal Lebonsky made lasagna because she said it was a special occasion since I don't come over that often anymore. She said it like she wanted me to feel bad about it.

I really wanted to ask her about the stuff that had been happening at school. Like if they had any suspects, and what the teachers and parents were saying about it. Then I started to worry that I might not be able to look innocent. Principal Lebonsky had a way of looking at you, like she could see inside you, and she didn't like what you had for lunch. She didn't mention the pranks, so I didn't, either.

Principal Lebonsky must have had spinach ready for the salad, because there was a lot of it in the lasagna. She tried to mix it up in the cheese, but it made a whole layer of stringy greenness. After dinner, Principal Lebonsky gave me a brownie with a scoop of ice cream. I looked at the bowl she put down in front of Hector, half expecting to see spinach salad, but she gave him a brownie and ice cream, too. It even looked about the same size. She got a bowl for herself and sat down. Then she asked me if I knew what the pickle club planned to make for the fair. Hector stabbed his spoon into his ice cream and wouldn't look at me.

"We haven't really found anything that we feel is . . . fair worthy," I said. "We're, uh, conducting more pickling research to find something just right. But, you know, nothing too crazy. We're still beginners." I took a big bite of ice cream that gave me brain freeze, but it stopped me from talking.

"You'd better get cracking. Pickles aren't like a box of that instant macaroni and cheese that you can just make at the last minute," she said. "They take time and care."

I apologized for disrespecting the pickle. "Have you considered eggs?" she said.

"On top of the pickles?" I asked. That picture of the pickled herring flashed in my head, but I pushed it out so I could keep eating my brownie.

"*As* the pickles, Ben. Surely a pickling fanatic like yourself must be familiar with pickled eggs."

I admitted I wasn't, and it made Principal Lebonsky's mouth look like she ate pickled lemon.

"I'll counsel Ms. Ruiz regarding her oversight. She should be advising you on all manner of preservable foods. We must be expected to respect customary traditions."

"I didn't know that anyone would want to pickle eggs."

"Oh, they are a delight. I used to make them in the summer, but they can stink up the apartment," she said. I think I remembered that. It smelled like a smoke bomb, but we're not allowed to have fireworks in our building.

Principal Lebonsky got a green recipe box down from the top of the refrigerator and flipped through the cards until she found the one she'd been looking for.

"Aha, my old recipe . . ." She handed me a wrinkled index card with a winking tomato in the corner. The recipe for "Lebonsky Eggs" was handwritten in perfect cursive letters. "Feel free to make it your own. Just stick with those ingredients and measurements. And instructions. They'll be perfect."

It kind of felt like an assignment, like now we had to make the principal's pickled eggs.

"The League of Pickle Makers had been talking about making some bread-and-butter pickles," I said. Principal Lebonsky nodded slowly.

"I'm sure that other groups will put together some bread-and-butter pickles," she said. "But those aren't quite up to our standards. Are they, Ben?"

"Are we done talking about the league of lint yet?" Hector said. He sighed and clanked his spoon down into his empty ice cream bowl.

"You would do well to join a club, Hector," Principal Lebonsky said. It wasn't the first time I'd heard her say it. The only sounds in the kitchen were the cat clock on the wall and me squirming in my chair. Hector just stared at the table. I stared at Hector at first, but then I stared at the table, too. I didn't say anything. Hector got up and left.

"Come on, Pickleboy," he called out from the living room.

There was a *Battlestar Galactica* marathon on TV. The original. It sounded like the perfect night to me because a) the original *Battlestar Galactica* is awesome, and b) they never, ever eat pickles on that show. No reminders about how much time I spent fake-making them.

31 We Pickle

"Hey, it's skinny Benny," Diego said when I walked into the restaurant on Saturday morning. He says it almost every time. Anybody else would bug me, but you can't be mad at Diego. "Que pasa? You eating first, or cleaning later?"

I have never seen him not laugh when he says this. Not even a fake laugh, either. He gives himself the giggles. He's been saying it ever since I started helping at the restaurant. Diego is the happiest guy I know. Just being around him makes me feel cool.

"Today, for you, *papas con crema*. Potatoes, cream, a little garlic, and chile. I'll teach you how to make it. Delicious, quick and easy." It would have been, too, if I hadn't spilled the cream in the walk-in. Diego didn't say anything, but I knew to move the mats, get a rag and some cleaner, and sop it up. If you want to make people in a restaurant mad, leave a mess for someone else to clean up. I did it once when I was seven. I spilled a bunch of sour cream down the back of the prep table and didn't say anything until it smelled funky and my mom forced a confession out of me. Being the owner's kid doesn't stop dirty looks.

"Hey, Diego. Maybe I could bring my friend Oliver sometime, and you could teach him to cook, too?" I said. Oliver baked great stuff in his tiny apartment. I bet he'd love to make something in a big restaurant kitchen. Diego said yes, like I knew he would.

I went into my parents' office to use the computer after we ate. I had an email from Ms. Ruiz. She said Principal Lebonsky had called her at home to say that she thought that it would be a good idea if the League of Pickle Makers were "responsible for providing a traditionally pickled egg befitting of, and demonstrating respect for, the pioneer way of life." Ms. Ruiz *never* talked like that.

So the League of Pickle Makers met to actually pickle stuff on Thursday. Over the weekend, I forwarded the email from Ms. Ruiz about the eggs to the pickle makers. Frank responded back with a link to the website. He'd set up a message board and a page to plug in prank information. If any of us had a message for the group, we could just send an email that said "Pickle." Then we'd know to go check the website and talk about stuff there. He said it made our communication more secure. I said it made it more awesome.

I brought the recipe card that Principal Lebonsky had given me to show the others. Bean had actually heard of pickled eggs before and got kind of excited about it. Oliver wasn't crazy about the idea at first, but Sienna talked him into it.

I had boiled a lot of eggs in one of the big pots we use to make menudo on Sundays, and I ran to the restaurant to get it. Diego had filled the pot with ice water to cool them off, so I just picked the whole thing up and lugged it to the lab. School had been over for ten minutes and the front of my shirt was wet by the time I got back. The door to the lab was shut, but I could hear Sienna's voice inside. I tapped it with the pot so someone would come and let me in. Every time I whacked the door, the eggs would do this cool drum roll rattle thing. I did it a few more times until I sloshed egg water into my eye. Then I set the pot down and opened the door myself. I brought the eggs in and closed the door behind me with my butt.

"That's not the kind of thing we do," Oliver said.

"Who says?" Sienna stood by Oliver with her hands on her hips. I stopped just past the doorway with the pot of eggs. Something told me we wouldn't be pickling yet.

"It's the rule. We already decided it. Only pranks that are fun or funny. That's just nasty."

"Well, I think it would be hilarious," said Sienna. "What do you think, Frank?"

Frank shrugged.

"I'm neutral. It's gross . . . but we'd definitely get a reaction," he said.

"What are you guys talking about?" I said. Oliver rolled his eyes and shook his head.

"Sienna wants to dump a bunch of plastic cockroaches in the cafeteria food," he said.

"That's pretty great, right? Right?! People would flip!" Sienna said. My stomach flipped.

"It's kind of messed up," I said. "And they'd probably just throw the food out and make everybody cheese sandwiches like they did when the freezer broke."

"Well, I like cheese sandwiches. And it's a lot better than the mystery nuggets that are on the menu tomorrow."

"It's a waste of food," I said. I scratched my nose and kept my eyes on the floor. I didn't want to talk about it.

"That's what you're worried about?" Oliver said. "Wasting food? No, I think there's a story here."

"Just drop it, okay?" I felt my cheeks burn and I knew I was blushing.

"Oh, I think Clevoliver is right," Bean said. "Ben's hiding something."

"Is it because your family has a restaurant?" Sienna said. "It's no big deal for the school."

"Spill it, Ben," Oliver said. "Are you afraid of a few little bugs?"

"I'm not afraid! It's just that roaches are gross, all right? I ate one once. By accident."

"Well, I for one am relieved to hear that it wasn't on purpose," Frank said.

"You guys can't tell anybody. I mean it!" They swore they wouldn't, and I took a deep breath. "We had them in the restaurant once. A long time ago when we first opened. My mom called an exterminator and nobody saw any for a few days. Then I snuck into the walk-in while my mom and dad were busy in the front to snack on some flan."

"What's flan?" Oliver said.

"It's like caramel pudding, or custard," I said.

"I'm simultaneously thrilled and horrified by where this is going."

"Shut up, Bean. The first couple of bites were smooth and creamy, just like it's supposed to be. But, then I took another bite. And it crunched. I knew right away. I spit it out, but I could still tell it was a roach. I threw up on the mat and told them I spilled some pea soup. I haven't eaten flan since." I hadn't told anybody about it ever. Just talking about it made my stomach clench up.

"That was a delight. Thank you, Ben." Bean clapped me on the back.

"Maybe we should vote," Oliver said. "Who's pro-bug?" Sienna raised her hand, like we didn't know already, and Oliver did, too. "Sorry, Ben. Okay, who is pro-nuggets?"

Bean and Frank raised their hands. Bean looked conflicted. I think she liked the idea of bugs, but not as much as she liked voting against Sienna.

"You're the tie-breaker, Ben." Sienna turned to me and smiled. "It could be really funny." She looked so hopeful. Her hair was pulled back into a loose ponytail, so I could see little gold hoops in her ears. And that lip gloss. But I couldn't forget the flan. So I shook my head, and the smile fell right off of her face.

"Maybe we could come up with something else to do in the cafeteria instead," I said. "I'm just not down with bugs."

"Whatever." Sienna swung her backpack off of the chair.

"Hey, what about the eggs?" I said. Sienna just sneered.

"I don't know why I agreed to join this stupid club anyway."

I wanted to tell her that she had *asked* to join the club, but I didn't. She pushed me out of the way to get out of the lab. Some water sloshed out of the pot onto the dull linoleum of the lab floor. Everyone was quiet.

"Wouldn't it have been easier to pour the water out before walking over here?" Oliver asked. Diego had said that the eggs were cooling off. It didn't occur to me to dump the water.

"Yeah, and it would have been easier if someone helped carry them, too," I said. I wanted to go after Sienna and find out what she was so mad about, but first I had to set down the pot of eggs. My feet didn't move.

"Geez, Ben. Did you even remember the jar?" Bean said.

"I'm holding it behind my back with my third arm." My face felt hot, and I kept picturing plastic bugs in food. It felt all wrong. Oliver crossed the lab and tugged the pot out of my hands. Egg water sloshed on my shoes.

"Let's get this over with." He grabbed a couple eggs and whacked the shells against the table. Bean and Frank peeled, too. They picked bits of shell off the eggs and made a pile of broken chips. Nobody talked.

I walked out into the hall, but Sienna was long gone. I didn't want to go back into the lab, so I ran back to the restaurant for the jar. I had put it through the dishwasher that makes everything smell like bleach, but it still smelled like chiles. Only parts of the label came off. Instead of "Green Comet Chiles" it said just "Come Chil."

When I came back, the peeled eggs were in the pot and the shells were in the trash, but everyone had left. I followed the recipe for Lebonsky Eggs and set the jar in the cupboard that Ms. Ruiz had reserved for us. I knew it was our cupboard by the "League of Pickle Makers Use Only!!" sign she'd made with permanent marker on green construction paper cut into what I assumed was supposed to be a pickle shape. She always told us to take it easy with the exclamation points. I guess she felt that some situations, like pickling space, called for more excitement.

El Matador

"When do we get to do something with costumes?" Oliver said. He looked at Bean. "You have a costume shop, right?"

"What are you talking about?" Sienna said. She sat with us in the cafeteria at lunch like nothing had happened. She seemed to be in a better mood, so I guess we all just decided to let it slide. I had brought a peanut butter sandwich from home, just in case. I reminded Sienna about Bean's family's store.

"I've got a pretty good idea of something we can do. And since I'm planning it, it will count as my solo mission," Bean said. "Ben wore a costume from the shop last year. Didn't you, Ben?" She didn't look at me, but she was smirking down at her burger. My mom and dad rented costumes from Lee's, before I knew it was Bean's store.

"What did you dress up as, Ben?" Sienna asked. Judging

from Bean's giggle, she remembered. I tried to think of a way to make it sound good.

"Last year my mom had a big party at the restaurant for Halloween," I said. "I work there sometimes." Sienna nodded, and I think she looked a little bit impressed. I took a deep breath. "She rented a fancy flamenco dancer costume, and my dad got a pirate costume. He put coal around his eyes and blackened his teeth. He looked pretty freaky."

"Cool," Sienna said. "What were you?"

I had really wanted to wear a shirt that said "Go, Ceilings!" so I could be a ceiling fan, but my mom said it would be good for business if I did something else. I thought she might rent a storm trooper costume, or maybe a samurai. A samurai would have been cool.

"You dressed up like a . . . matador, didn't you?" Bean said.

"A minotaur? The bull man?" Frank said.

"A *mat-a-dor.* Bullfighter. Ben looked pretty cool." I looked up at Bean as she dipped a French fry into a glob of ketchup and popped it into her mouth. She was lying.

If you're lucky enough not to be familiar with the ridiculous uniform of the matador, let me tell you about it. Lee's version of an authentic matador costume had short, tight, bright purple pants. I could stop right there and you would already feel sorry for me. But, it gets worse. The pants had wide shiny gold strips of lace sewn down the sides. They buttoned just below the knees with a big gold button. What else?

Red socks and black ballet slippers. With bells. I told my mom that I didn't think matadors wore bells, but she said not to take them off because she didn't want to lose her deposit. It came with a puffy shirt and a jacket with big shoulder pads. Not like football shoulder pads. Gold lace shoulder pads. With pom-poms. And a hat shaped like a pot sticker.

I told my dad I looked silly. He said I didn't have a choice and to quit being such a *sabelotodo*, which is Spanish for smart aleck. He said that matadors were brave men of honor. I said that I would need to be brave to wear the matador costume to the restaurant.

The jacket was so stiff I couldn't lift my arms enough to bus tables. No way could I fight a bull. I whined to my mom and she said to stop before I got food on it. I thought I was off the hook, but I wasn't. She told me to walk around the restaurant to make nice with everybody and pass roses out to the ladies. I wondered if my mom loved me at all.

An old lady said I was the handsomest matador she'd ever seen and kissed me on both cheeks. I felt like a fool.

I figured that whatever I wound up wearing for a prank, it

couldn't be any worse than that matador getup. Maybe I'd get to be a zombie after all.

"Let's do it this weekend," Bean said. "I'll get everything together and let you guys know where to meet."

"That's what I'm talking about." Frank nodded. "It's time we branched out a little bit. Got away from the school. We need to take it to the streets." Everybody yelled and high fived, but I still needed to know a little more about exactly *what* we'd be taking to the streets.

"What does that mean exactly?" I said.

"It means we're expanding our turf. Pushing the envelope off of school grounds," Frank said.

"There's a big difference, a *huge* difference, between getting busted by Principal Lebonsky and getting caught by the police," I said.

"I'd rather get caught by the police," Bean mumbled.

"We're not going to get caught," Oliver said. "Not if we play our parts well."

"You don't know," I said. "I feel funny about doing something that's not just goofing off at school."

"It will be fun, Ben," Bean said. "Don't freak, all right?"

"What about the P.T.A. cards?" Oliver asked.

"Forget the P.T.A. cards," I said.

"How will we get credit?" Frank said. I shook my head.

"This one's got to be anonymous," I said. "Just for a laugh."

"Everything will be cool, Ben. No weird stuff," Bean said.

"Do you promise?"

Bean said she did. Then she held out her hand to shake on it. I was about to shake, but then she spit on her palm—or did a really good job pretending to spit on it. I didn't want her to tell the pickle makers any more about the matador costume, so I shook anyway.

Bad Eggs

"Taste one," Oliver said.

"No way." The jar was still in the cupboard, but the eggs inside looked like eyeballs in swamp juice. The vinegar had turned a cloudy green, and the herbs in the bottom looked rotten.

"We need to know if they're any good," Bean said.

"It's a pickled egg. It's not going to be any good," Frank said.

"Well, we can't enter them in the pickling contest if they stink," Sienna said. She pulled them down out of the cupboard and spun the lid open. They did stink. Literally. Opening the lid was like setting off a stink bomb. Kids in the hall started complaining right away. It was pickley vinegar, sure, but there was something else there. Like when I left half a burrito in the car all weekend during a heat wave.

"Whatever. I'll try one, you chickens." Frank dunked his hand into the jar, making the eggs and herb flecks swirl around. We weren't getting any points for hygiene.

"What the—" Frank dropped the egg he had snagged out of the jar and it clacked down onto the table.

"That one is fake!" He pulled a couple more out. Once they were out of the pickle juice, it was easy to see that they were the kind of plastic Easter eggs that broke in half.

"Real funny, guys. Where are the real ones?" I said, but everyone looked as confused as I was. We poured the rest of the jar into the sink.

"Who would do this?" Oliver said, sorting through the pile of eggs.

Twenty-two eggs, and not a real one in the bunch. The pickle juice had turned them all a yellowish gray.

"What are we going to take to the fair?" Sienna said.

"Forget the fair, what kind of sicko would steal our eggs?" Oliver said.

"Maybe somebody else in the pickle contest?" Bean guessed.

"Would someone really care that much about a ribbon from the Pioneer Fair?" Oliver said.

"Don't forget about the cash prize," I said.

"Ah, cash. It corrupts us all," Frank said. We all looked at him, and then back to the eggs. Oliver held one up to the sunlight shining in through the lab window.

"Wait—there's something inside this," he said. He tried to crack an egg open, but it slipped out of his hand. Frank grabbed it and set it on the table and whacked it with my math book. Broken bits of plastic sprayed out, and a folded piece of paper stuck to the table.

> **If you want your eggs back, you have to let me in the club.**
> **—Hector**

We stared at the note. Frank's mouth hung open and his eyes were a little buggy. For once, he didn't look cool.

"I didn't see that coming," Oliver said. We opened more eggs, but they all had the same note. Hector wasn't taking any chances.

"I didn't know he had it in him," Bean said. It sounded

like it was a compliment. I looked back and forth between her and Hector's note. I didn't know which one was a bigger surprise.

"Well, I guess there's only one thing to do," Oliver said.

"Find him and knock him out?" Bean said.

"No."

"Break into his apartment. Find our eggs. Steal them back," Frank said.

"What? No, maybe we just invite him to join the club," Oliver said.

"Are you crazy? Then he'll find out about the P.T.A.," Bean said.

"Maybe that would be okay, too," Oliver said.

"You've got to admit, this was slick. He's got style," Frank said. Oliver and Bean stared at me, and Frank and Sienna stared at the sink full of plastic eggs. I didn't say anything. I hadn't expected Hector to try and join the club, and I'd been so caught up in the excitement that I hadn't really thought about it too much since the start. It would've been okay with me, really, but doing it without Hector was okay, too. The risk of getting busted was just too high. And I'm not just talking about myself. I looked around at them. I didn't know Frank or Sienna last year at all because they weren't at my school. I barely knew Oliver, and all right, I was afraid of Bean. But now the five of us were the League of Pickle Makers. And the P.T.A. And I'd sworn to keep it secret.

We set out to look for Hector, and we found him fifty feet away. He was sitting on the floor in the hall. He'd actually replaced the eggs right after our last meeting and had been waiting a week for us to catch on and contact him.

"Whoa. I thought, like, you guys would figure it out right away the first time you tested the pickling solution," he said. "My grandma checks the solution all the time on her eggs." Sienna shook her head.

"Talk to Ben," Frank said, and left with the rest of the club.

I looked down at Hector. He just looked back at me like he didn't know where he knew me from.

"Where are our eggs?"

"I have them at home. I'm storing them in my bedroom in my grandma's pickling crock," he said. I started to ask him what a pickling crock was, but I didn't really want to know. "If you bring a jar over, you can have them back. She'll probably want to use her crock soon."

"Hector . . . you can't be in the club," I said. "It just wouldn't work."

"Why not? It could be fun."

"Pickle making?" I couldn't believe it. Even a kid who doesn't like pickles wanted to do it. I was *lousy* at making a bad club. "You don't even like pickles. Why would you want to make them?"

"I just want to hang out," Hector said. He scraped a scuff

mark on the wall with his fingernail. "Aren't we friends anymore?"

"Of course we're friends, but it doesn't mean we have to do *everything* together all the time. People change," I said.

"So, what, I'm not ALLOWED to join your club?"

"I just don't think it's a good idea. But, we can still hang out. I *want* to hang out."

"Now?" Hector said. "Want to come over and get the eggs?" He said it like he'd still hang out, even after I told him he couldn't be a pickle maker. It made me feel like a dirt sandwich.

"No, not now. I need to go help Diego," I said.

"Fine. Nice knowing you." Hector got up and slung his backpack over his shoulder. He stomped down the hall to his grandma's office, where he knew I wouldn't follow him.

Sitting Fine on the Good Laws of Finland

From: Agent Super
To: Agent Fix-it; Agent 008; Agent Queso; Agent Snow
I have a plan. It's not illegal. I'll bring supplies. Details here: Pickle.

I went to the website, but her message was in a different language. It took me forever to figure out that it was in Finnish, and I'm not sure the translator was so hot.

Agent Super: Operation Zoo Escape Plan is had that sits fine on good law. Masquerade clothing be already on place for you chosen. Local bird toilets, Saturday, 11

Sienna posted a reply right away in French.

Agent Snow: Saturday at eleven is when my dad calls, and he's been talking about coming to visit, so I'll miss it.☹

The frowny face was the same in English and French. I noticed that she didn't ask to reschedule it or anything. I think that the zoo prank made her nervous, too. Right away Frank posted. I was starting to get used to everyone's agent names. It was in English.

Agent Fix-it: Everybody can just say what they have to say. No need to change the language. The CIA couldn't even hack this.

We can take care of business without Agent Snow. I'm sure she can think of a makeup assignment. Peace.

Since everybody seemed to be online, I posted, too.

Agent Queso: Our eggs are safe at Hector's. I'll have them back in the pickle makers' cupboard ASAP. Messing around at the zoo could be fun, but nobody from school will even see it. Maybe it's not worth it?

I refreshed the page until there was a new response. Bean.

Agent Super: We're doing it for fun. Lighten up, birdbrain.

No help there. I went into the living room and asked my dad if he needed help in the restaurant on Saturday. He didn't.

Zoo Break

I logged into my email first thing on Saturday morning, sort of hoping that someone had called off the prank. Nobody from the P.T.A. had sent anything, but there was an email from Hector.

> Wanna come pick up the eggs? We could hang out. I have to go to the salad bar with my grandma for lunch, but I'm here before that. —H

If I had plans with Hector, I wouldn't have to do the zoo prank, whatever it was. But, I didn't say anything the other day so they'd know it was more about having chicken parts than meet-up plans.

```
Sorry. Already have plans today.
—Ben
```

I checked my email after breakfast. Still nothing from the pickle makers. Or Hector, not that I gave him much to respond to. It was time to face the costumes.

I was ten minutes late, but I found Oliver waiting alone for me in front of the bathroom near the Domestic Birds of America exhibit. It was the perfect place for a secret rendezvous, because it was the most deserted corner of the zoo. Oliver held out a plastic bag from Lee's.

"Where's your costume?" I said.

"Frank's got it inside. He's changing and Bean's in there, too," he said.

"In the boys' room?"

"Yeah, but you can change in the stall."

"What am I?"

"You're an animal," he said and threw the bag at me. We went into the bathroom and found Frank in a lion suit. The suit hung over his skinny body, but the face was pretty good. If he hammed it up, he could make it work. Bean stood there in her green overalls.

"Where's *your* costume?"

"I don't have one. Think of me as your animal trainer. If we were all in costumes, it might get too confusing," she said. "Although, I really thought about wearing the army captain uniform today. Alas, I need to blend in." She shook her head sadly.

"Here, you can take mine. I'll be the 'animal trainer.' "

"No. I brought them, you wear them. This is *my* prank, remember?"

"Then you might want to think about doing it alone," I said.

"Like you did that awesome cloud of gloom alone?"

"Well, if we're the ones wearing the costumes, we're the ones that could get busted. I don't see how this counts as an initiation for you," I said.

"Good point, Ben," Oliver said.

"I'm totally taking the risk! If you bozos get caught, you know what they're going to find? 'Property of Lee's Costume' sewn into your mangy collars. My dad will know I took the costumes. All of the risk is on me. Mostly," Bean said.

"Fine. Is torturing us part of your secret plan?"

"Yes."

"What is your plan, anyway?"

"I'm going to keep it simple." She paused for effect and looked around. "You boys are going to run around until we scare someone."

It didn't sound like much of a plan, but then again, it wasn't so bad if we could leave as soon as we freaked someone out.

"Can we leave right after we scare someone?"

"Sure, Ben," Bean said. "And make it snappy, because the costumes have to be back by three for the Bernstein-Miller wedding."

I studied her face to tell if she was lying or not. But she just smiled and strolled casually out of the restroom. I knew we were in for trouble. I went into a stall to put my costume on. Not because I was shy, but just in case some pigeon fanatic came in to pee.

I tried to tell what Oliver was from what I could see of his legs under the stall walls, but I could only see brown fur. I pulled my own costume out.

"What is this, Frank?" I said.

"Dunno," Frank said. "Bean wouldn't let us peek."

Oliver's legs were light brown, but my costume was more of a reddish brown. It was a tight squeeze in the stall. I took off my T-shirt and shorts. I didn't want Bean to do something stupid like try and take a picture of me in my underwear to put online, so I pulled the suit on as fast as I could. The very tip of a big, fluffy tail dipped into the toilet, but it was only in there for a second.

Okay, that's a lie. The whole end went in, and it swished around a little bit before I noticed because I was pulling up the padded stomach and squeezing my arms into the holes as fast as I could. I tried to dry off the tail with some toilet paper, but the tissue just fell apart, so I grabbed a couple of toilet seat covers.

"What are you doing in there?" Oliver yelled over the wall. "Are you dressed yet?"

"Almost," I said.

"What's all the crackling paper? Dude, are you going to the *bathroom*?"

"No!" I said. I gave up on the soggy tail, threw the seat covers into the toilet and flushed.

"Dude. You *were* going to the bathroom. This isn't number two time, it's showtime," Oliver said.

"Don't give him grief," Frank said. "When you have to go, you go. Ben, you could have told us. We would have waited. Outside."

"I WASN'T pooping!" I said, and squeezed out of the stall.

I could see myself in the dirty mirror. I had a furry beige potbelly. A big fluffy tail swung out behind me, dripping toilet water. The whole thing itched.

I took the head out of the bag. Big eyes. Big, buck teeth and pointy ears. I put my clothes into the plastic bag. Oliver came out of his stall. He was a bear with long pointy teeth and shaggy, matted fur. He'd make a pretty good grizzly, if a grizzly bear had a high-pitched laugh. I looked in the mirror over the sinks.

"I am a giant squirrel," I whispered. I looked pretty lifelike, besides the jumbo factor.

"*Squirrelus giganticus*!" Frank said. Bean came back in and laughed so hard she almost fell backward into the trash can. I wish she had.

"I can't go out there like this," I said. "There's no such thing as a giant squirrel." Frank grabbed my bag of clothes and passed it to Oliver, who ran outside with it. It dawned on me too late that I could have put the costume on *over* my clothes. Then I wondered how often the costumes got washed. It didn't smell like it was very often. Maybe other people changed in bathrooms and parts fell into the toilet. I felt ill.

"You're a new species. Just discovered," Frank said. "Let's go!" He ran out of the bathroom growling.

The idea was for Frank, Oliver, and me to dash around like we were escaping. If we got separated, we would meet up later on the sidewalk outside the side entrance. Bean's job

My lungs felt too small. I had to get out. I crawled out of the bushes on all fours. I really needed to tell the others that I was going home. And that's when things got weird.

Out of the tiny squirrel eyeholes I saw the fender of a big rig, speeding right toward my squirrel nose.

"Sheep!" I heard the driver yell, but it wasn't *exactly* "sheep." And it wasn't a big rig. It was one of those zoo golf carts. He swerved around me and hit the trash cans, and that made Frank and Oliver jump out. They disappeared into the bamboo stuff, which made the driver yell "Sheep!" again, but it wasn't sheep that time, either. I jumped up when the zoo guy tried to reverse the cart, but it was stuck on the curb. He unlatched his seat belt and sort of tumble-crawled out of his seat to the back of the cart, where he opened a big toolbox-type thing.

"Run!" Bean yelled. "RUN!" She was already halfway to the Primate Plaza.

I ran, screaming, down the path, which apparently is what we should have done in the first place if we wanted to freak out the zoogoers. I slammed straight into a pack of people watching the chimpanzees pick bugs off each other.

The cart driver yelled something, but I couldn't hear him through my padded head. I kept screaming, and the people all started shouting and screaming, too. They jumped out of the way, and took off in the opposite direction down the path. I don't know if they were running from me, or the freaked-out zoo guy.

I stopped to look for Frank and Oliver, but they were nowhere around. Bean ran right into me, literally, which got my attention, because everyone else was moving away from me. She looked at me over her shoulder as she ran past into the Bat House, carrying the plastic bag my costume came in. The bag with my clothes. I followed her into the Bat House, and squeezed through as the doors closed behind me. The zoo guy stopped on the path, looking wobbly and green through the tinted glass. He held a walkie-talkie up to his mouth. He wasn't coming in, but he wasn't going away, either.

"What are we going to do?" I said, as Zoo Guy stopped a couple of people from coming into the Bat House. Another golf cart pulled up and the first zoo guy grabbed a bullhorn off the seat. More people tried to come in, but they were stopped like the others. A crowd gathered around the carts.

"ATTENTION, GUESTS CURRENTLY ENJOYING THE BAT HOUSE. THERE IS SOMEONE—OR SOMETHING—ODD WITH YOU IN THE BAT HOUSE. PLEASE LEAVE IN AN ORDERLY FASHION. IMMEDIATELY."

"Get dressed. Quick!" Bean threw the bag at me and turned around. I got out of the squirrel suit a lot quicker than I had gotten into it. I put my clothes back on and looked around, but Bean had disappeared behind me through the dark tunnel that led to the bat cavern. Just as I buttoned up my pants, a family ran past toward the doors with Bean right behind them. I shoved the squirrel suit back in the bag. Bean crouched down to whisper into my ear. "This is the only way out. I checked. Come on, it's time to panic."

We ran out of the bat house together screaming. I realized I sounded a lot like me as the squirrel, so I tried to scream a little deeper.

Zoo Guy stood in front of the crowd with the bullhorn, and two more zookeepers had joined him. One held a weird-looking gun, and the other two talked into walkie-talkies. I wondered if they were talking to each other, just trying to look cool, but then it dawned on me that they might have called the police.

"HELP! It's back there in the bat house. It's terrible!" I yelled. Bean made some blubbering noises, which I thought sounded fake, but she had real tears squirting. The zoo guys all started shouting questions, but we acted like we were too scared to stay anywhere close to the Bat House and ran away.

We didn't slow down until we were through the side gate. Frank and Oliver, out of their costumes, were waiting for us under the "Get Wild This Summer!" banner. They were just looking like normal everyday kids standing around on the street holding plastic bags full of fur and rubber. Sienna was with them, too.

"Hey, I thought you were staying home to talk to your dad," I said.

"I guess he was busy." Sienna shrugged and looked down the street. "I came over here to see if you needed help and found these guys coming out. Did you get the eggs back yet?"

"I'll get them later," I said. I nodded toward Frank and Oliver. "How'd it go with you guys?"

Frank and Oliver worried about getting caught, so they headed straight back to the Birds of America bathroom and took the costumes off. Those braniacs had just put the costumes on over their clothes, so they didn't have to get naked in public. Genius. We took a vote, and agreed there would be no more missions requiring the use of big furry costumes. It was unanimous.

"Not bad, but this doesn't get you in the club, *Margaret*." I ducked out of the way of her fist.

"As if! I'm totally a member, Diaz," Bean said.

"I'm with Ben," Oliver said. "We took all the risk in there."

"You guys were hiding in the toilet stalls! Ben and I were the ones dodging tranquilizer darts."

"Wait, they tried to *tranquilize* you?" Oliver said. I shook my head.

"They totally could have. Back me up, Frank," Bean said.

"I'm going with Ben on this one. But we all have faith that you'll come up with something Beany," Frank said. He put his hand on her shoulder, but she shrugged it off. She grabbed the costume bags and glared at us.

"Sorry about the tail. How often do you clean these anyway?"

"What?"

"How often do you clean the costumes?"

"What?"

"The costumes. Not to be rude, but they don't seem very clean," I said. Bean held her hand up to her ear and shook her head like she couldn't hear me. I was pretty sure I had my answer, so I gave up and walked home.

The Next Twenty Minutes

I really just wanted to go home, relax, and read a book in something non-itchy before I had to be at Lupe's, but it wasn't over yet. I opened the front door to my building and found Hector standing in front of the mailboxes with his arms crossed and his feet wide. Like he expected someone to try to shove him over.

"Just say it, Ben."

The lobby is more like a wide hall with just enough room for mailboxes and peeling wallpaper before you get to the stairs. I couldn't really get up to my apartment without pushing Hector out of the way. He looked like he wanted me to push him so he could push back.

"Hey, is it a good time to come up and get the eggs?" I said. He just glared at me. I sighed. "What do you want me to say, Hector?"

"Say you're done being friends with me. You only want to hang out with your cool, new friends—fine by me. But have the guts to say it to my face."

"Hector, I'm not in the mood," I said. I tried to go around him, but he moved to block my way. "Look, you don't understand. There are things I can't tell you."

"Because you're a coward."

"Because they are secret!"

"Oh, I already know your mom uses salsa from jars at the restaurant," he said.

"She does not. Take it back." Hector just glared at me. "Take it back now, Hector."

"Forget it. Why don't you have her sell the stupid pickles you're always making with your precious club? Huh?" He pushed my shoulder. I felt the top of my head getting hot and my fingers tingled. "Your pickles are probably so gross, your own mom wouldn't eat them."

"You know why you can't be in the pickle club, Hector? Because you can't keep a secret. If you knew what happened in pickle club, you'd go tell your grandma."

"I would not."

"Well, they all think you would," I said. Hector flinched.

"What do *you* think?" He glared at me.

"I think you tattled to your grandma about something somebody *else* drew on the building. Something I got in trouble for!"

"I said I was sorry," Hector said.

"That wasn't the only time! Don't you remember when Bean stuck gum under the desk? You told on her and she got in trouble. She had to scrape gum out from under all the tables, and a lot of that wasn't even hers."

"That happened almost a year ago! I haven't told on anybody since," he yelled.

"They don't trust you!" It felt too warm in the hall. "You've got to grow up and stop worrying if you're doing things your mean old grandma's way. I'm doing things *my* way. With kids who don't care what the principal will say about it. It's not like we're hurting anybody."

Hector shook his head and turned toward the stairs.

"Have a nice life," he said.

It only took me seven steps to crack. If I ever want to join the C.I.A. or something, all they have to do is ask Hector about this particular incident. They'll see that I take pressure like a wet noodle. I felt like I was going to explode before he got to the first landing.

"We don't make pickles. Not really. We only made the pickled eggs for the fair," I said. Hector stopped, but he didn't turn around. "We pull pranks. Like the balls, and the party, and the foam in the fountains. That was all us. And it's SECRET. It's a SECRET CLUB. If your grandma found out we would all be in serious trouble. Just for having a little fun. And if you were there, you would *tell* her about us. You'd get punished. I'd get punished. And the rest of them, too. You probably wouldn't think what we do was fun anyway. Don't you understand?" I couldn't get enough air. My hands balled into white-knuckled fists.

"Why do you do it then?" Hector turned around. "If so many people could get in so much trouble, why do you keep doing it?"

"Because sometimes life should just be fun, Hector," I said. "We shouldn't have to worry about what teachers and parents and *principals* tell us to do every second of every day! When do we get to choose? I'm choosing now."

"You don't have to do stuff like that just to impress your new friends. Just be yourself."

"I'm not trying to impress anybody! I'm making my *own* choices. To have fun. My way. People don't even know it's us," I said, but he was already shaking his head.

"I already guessed you were the one doing that stuff. Jerk." His words fell down the stairs and landed on my chest.

"Come on, Hector. Don't go away mad. Can I at least get our eggs?" I don't think he heard me over the door slamming.

37
Just a Second

I know what you are thinking.

You think I should have kept my big yap shut and not told Hector about the club. Right? I'm in trouble, and the pickle makers are right there with me. This is going to be so much worse than The Graffiti Incident. I can't really think of any instances since then, when I know for sure that Hector spilled the beans, but let's just say there have been suspicious circumstances. Principal Lebonsky is not psychic, but she knows things. Unless she's got an army of eavesdroppers, my guess is she's getting her information from Hector. I'm not the only one who thinks so.

Loyalty is everything. I'm loyal. At the restaurant, the guys in the kitchen do all kinds of crazy stuff, and I never tell. Besides, if I did, they'd probably stop teaching me how to insult people in Spanish. And then they'd start telling on me when

I hid out in the kitchen telling jokes or eating *tres leches* cake in the walk-in, instead of busing tables or whatever gross thing they have me doing. My life would be ruined.

What am I saying? If Hector tells his grandma about the P.T.A., then we will all be in a big world of Lebonsky hurt. My life *will* be ruined. I will have no friends. Sure, people will admire me from afar, but if I don't have Hector *or* the pickle makers, I'll have to hang out with Finn Romo, and he talks about what his pet lizards are doing way too much. All of my real friends will be gone, and who can blame them.

So, let's recap. A week until the Pioneer Fair, and we have no pickles. Or pickled things. Or time to make pickled things. We would have had the principal's pickled eggs, but Hector stole them.

My oldest friend, Hector Lebonsky, hates me. I can feel it coming up through the squeaky floorboards with his grandma's cooking smells. Cabbage soup and loathing. Marinara with a side of rage. Oatmeal and animosity.

We are not getting our eggs back.

We are doomed. Hector is going to tell Principal Lebonsky everything.

Are we all caught up now? Great. Moving on.

Extreme Volleyball

"CAN YOU HEAR ME? IS THIS LOUD ENOUGH? THERE'S A NOTE HERE FROM THE P.T.A. THAT THERE'S A PROBLEM WITH THE MICROPHONE AND WE NEED TO SPEAK AS LOUDLY AS POSSIBLE." Pat, the secretary, shrieked from the P.A. speakers through the gym. Most kids covered their ears. Except Bean. She was smiling as she unzipped her hoodie. She held it open and smirked at me.

"I'M OFFICIAL NOW, CHUMPS!" was written across the front of her T-shirt in red, iron-on block letters. She'd drawn what looked like a pickle sticking its tongue out underneath to drive home the message. Probably with the same marker that she had used for the note on the intercom. She marched over to Oliver and Frank and showed them, too. No points for subtlety. Frank gave her a thumbs-up.

"THERE WILL BE AN ASSEMBLY ON THE RAINBOW

OF PROPER NUTRITION ON MONDAY. OH, AND DON'T FORGET TO BRING DONATIONS FOR THE BAKE SALE MONDAY. BAKE! SALE! MONDAY! AND THE PIONEER FAIR IS THIS SATURDAY MORNING. COME ONE, COME ALL FOR A TRIP THROUGH HISTORY! PARTICIPATING CLUBS ARRIVE AT TEN TO SET UP. DOORS OPEN FOR STUDENTS AND THE GENERAL PUBLIC AT ELEVEN. ELEVEN!"

The speaker clicked off. Coach Capell blew the whistle for extreme volleyball. It was sort of like regular volleyball, but with no net. And tackling. Standing still wasn't advised. It's not really the place to be thinking about the Pioneer Fair, either. I got knocked down six times.

Emergency Meeting

"We don't have any pickles for the Pioneer Fair," I said. The P.T.A. sat in the back booth at Lupe's. I was technically supposed to be helping out in the kitchen, but I was taking a break for a "school project."

"What if we did something else at the fair?" Bean said.

"Like what?" Oliver said.

"You know . . ." Bean whispered. "A prank."

The idea of a prank at the fair had occurred to me, but I hadn't thought of anything really fantastic that we could do yet.

"No," Sienna said.

"No?!" Bean put her eyebrows up, like she dared Sienna to say it again.

"I mean, *please* no. Could we skip it? I think my dad is coming to visit, and I don't want anything to mess it up,"

Sienna said. Bean went back to rearranging the salt and pepper shakers with the flowers my dad puts on the tables.

"That's all right with me," I said. "We'll skip the fair as the P.T.A. But, what are we going to do as the League of Pickle Makers?"

"We *totally* need to make something great," Sienna said. "Something my dad would like!" I really wanted to think of something great that Sienna's dad would like. Diego brought some *pan dulce* and *horchata* out of the kitchen. He used the big glasses, because my mom and dad weren't around.

"Well, I'm not sure what kind of pickles we can make in four days," I said.

Oliver sat up and faced Diego. "Can you make *escabeche*?"

"Of course I can." Diego looked offended.

"Can you show us? Like, teach us how to do it?" Oliver asked.

"Sure, if you guys wanna learn."

"What's *escabeche*?" Frank said.

"It's spicy carrots and onions and stuff that my mom gives out with chips and salsa after people order," I said. "That stuff." I pointed to the jar on the table.

"It's *pickled* vegetables. They're pickles!" Oliver practically shouted. "Can we have them ready in three days?"

"It's better if they cure longer, but sure, they'd still be good. I bet they'd win your contest. You guys eat some *pan dulce* while I get the stuff ready. Just give me a minute," Diego said.

"Nice one, Clevoliver. But wait, they didn't have Mexican restaurants in pioneer days," Bean said. "The judges aren't going to accept it." I thought about it.

"What if there were Mexican pioneers?" I said. "I bet there were."

"I've never seen any in the pictures. It's always just a bunch of white guys," Oliver said.

"It doesn't mean that they weren't there," I said. "Hang on, I'll be right back." I went into the back office where my mom writes the checks and stuff. I sat down at her computer and started searching. I couldn't find any Mexicans anywhere, and I got nervous, until I got a hit on the third page of results. I tapped the print button and ran back to the table.

"Some of the first city settlers were migrants from Mexico," I said. I felt kind of proud. I knew that my mom's family came from Los Angeles and my dad's parents were in Durango, Mexico, so the settlers didn't really have anything to do with me. But, it still made me feel good that they were there. I thought about Mrs. Wentworth, my old kindergarten teacher. She made me do my Thanksgiving pilgrim puppet over because I had used the

brown construction paper she'd set out for the Native American puppets. Turns out, there were brown pilgrims after all. For a minute I got worried that the others might not want to make a Mexican version of pickles. But, everyone was on board. I actually felt excited about pickling.

"Won't Principal Lebonsky get mad that we're not making eggs?" Oliver said. "And what about Ms. Ruiz? She said to pick a recipe out of her book."

"They'll probably be upset," Bean said. She smiled.

"I don't care what Principal Lebonsky says, but I hope Ms. Ruiz doesn't take it too hard. She gets really excited about pickles," I said. No one believed me.

"We don't have to do what they say all the time," I said. "This is *our* club." We went into the kitchen, and Diego got down to business giving us the what's what on chopping and measuring. Oliver asked him a lot of questions, so it took a while. We boiled carrots, onions, jalapenos, and tomatillos

in vinegar, and I threw in some of the pickling spice from the jar in my backpack. Diego told us to add some oregano and a little bit of cumin, and then Bean threw in some cilantro. I added garlic, because everything is better with garlic, and we poured it all into jars. Diego got all fancy and dipped the jars into boiling water with tongs to get the lids sucked on to keep out germs.

My mom and dad came in just as the pickle makers were leaving, and we showed them what we had made. We had two jars of mild *escabeche*, and two jars of hot. Sienna carried them in an old tomato box.

"My dad would love this. He really likes Mexican food. I bet he would like Lupe's, too," Sienna said. "I'm totally going to bring him here when he visits!"

"You bring him down for dinner. It will be our treat," my mom said.

"Thanks, Mrs. Diaz!" Sienna said.

"Our pleasure. You guys did good, *m'ijo*! That *escabeche* looks great. I'm so proud of you!" She gave me a big hug and a kiss in front of everyone, leaving her crazy red lipstick on my cheek. But, I didn't care.

We had pickles for the fair, and they were pickles to be proud of.

40 The Day Before

"Are you all set for tomorrow?" Ms. Ruiz leaned forward over the big bowl on her desk. It was like the crystal one that my mom kept mints in by the cash register, but a lot bigger.

"I think so, yeah," I said. I worried that she'd be mad that we didn't have the eggs. Maybe Principal Lebonsky would be mad at Ms. Ruiz, like it was her fault that we hadn't followed orders. "I wanted to talk to you about that. We've been working on something pretty unique."

"Do *not* tell me! I want to be surprised tomorrow when I see your creation. In this." She slid the big bowl across her desk toward me and smiled.

"Is this a pickle bowl?" I said. Ms. Ruiz laughed like I just asked her why six was afraid of seven.

"No, it's a punch bowl. It was my grandmother's, but I don't use it much. You could bring it tomorrow to display your lovely pickles." I couldn't really picture the *escabeche* in the bowl. We could mix up the mild and the spicy to fill it up, but it just seemed kind of fancy. I don't know what kind of pickles she thought would look better in a bowl like this, but I was really glad that we didn't go with the pickled pig feet recipe from *The Joy of Pickling*.

"Did the pioneers have punch bowls?"

"I'm sure they carried many beloved family heirlooms on the trail. Carefully."

Ms. Ruiz loved the bowl. Message received. I lifted it slowly off of the desk and promised to be extra careful with it. It made me kind of nervous, and I didn't really want to take it, but I didn't think I could say no. She was still watching me, so I wrapped my sweatshirt around it carefully for extra padding. I wanted to warn her that we were doing something different than what she expected. It looked like she had her hopes up.

"Ms. Ruiz, we used a different recipe than we first planned. Instead of the—"

"I don't need the details." She held up a hand. "I'll just wait and be surprised tomorrow."

Oh, crust. That's what I was afraid of.

Pioneer Preparations

I woke up early with a nervous stomach, so I had plenty of time to think about the fair. I still forgot Ms. Ruiz's punch-bowl and had to run back to my apartment. I grabbed some corn chips that the judges could eat with the *escabeche*, if they wanted to. There were a lot more school buses than normal. They must have brought the other schools' clubs. Crowds of kids walked toward the gym carrying their pioneer projects. Knitted stuff, patchwork blankets, something that I could only hope was some kind of beef jerky . . . I couldn't believe how many kids were into this. Sienna and Oliver were already standing by the gym doors. They were far away, but I could see that Sienna looked upset. She tried to wipe her face, but she was holding a box. Oliver reached out and wiped her cheek off with a handkerchief from his shirt pocket. For real. I can't believe that guy carries a handkerchief.

Frank had been in charge of getting the *escabeche* out of the cupboard in the lab, and he stood waiting with Bean by the fountain. Bean noticed me looking at them and held up a Lee's Costume & Party bag with supplies she'd snagged from the store. Frank held up the *escabeche*. We were all set.

"Exciting day, huh?" Leo stood beside me. Maybe he really liked pickles, too. But Leo never tried to join the club, so he must have been talking about something else.

I just nodded and walked toward the gym. A couple of eighth graders passed carrying big, golden pies. The crust twisted around the top, fancy-style, and bits of apple and berry poked up through the little holes. They looked pretty good and they smelled even better. If we were competing against pies, we were doomed.

Coach Capell and Rick had put up dividers so that the gym was split into four sections. The Foods of Yore Pavilion was in the back. There was also the Colonist Craft Coliseum, Pioneer Playfield, and History of the Homesteaders Center. A woman wearing a sunbonnet walked toward the History of the Homesteaders Center carrying a pile of brown furs. Another woman with a long dress and an apron led a goat past with a yellow ribbon around his neck. I didn't know what I had gotten myself into.

Only the clubs and people with exhibits were allowed in the gym at the start to get ready. We found our table in the corner. Bean had brought a tablecloth with horseshoes and tumbleweeds all over it. Probably not so great for a birthday party, but kind of super for a pioneer fair. We mixed the mild and spicy *escabeche* together in Ms. Ruiz's punch bowl and put some chips on a plate beside the bowl. We spread out some napkins and little paper bowls. The napkins had horseshoes and the bowls were plain white. Bean had really pulled through. It looked classy and pioneer-ish, if something can be both of those things at once. Sienna had written the recipe for the *escabeche* on a blue card and glued it to the green banner with my Mexican settler article. She hung it on the front of the table. Oliver brought some salad tongs. He said he knew that we wouldn't think about how people would get the *escabeche* without using their fingers. He was right.

"I'm going to throw the trash away and check out the exhibits," Sienna said. She grabbed a box from under the table and left. She still looked upset, and she didn't invite anyone to go with her.

"Has anyone tasted this stuff? To see if it's any good?" Bean asked. We hadn't. They wanted me to try it, but I thought we should all sample it. It was too late if the *escabeche* was nasty, but at least we would know. It tasted like sour chile garlic. I know it sounds weird, but it was kind of delicious. Bean and Oliver stopped after one bite, but Frank and I had some more with chips. Then Frank made me stop eating for a minute so that he could take pictures for the pickle page of the website. Good thinking.

We walked around to check out the competition. The other displays in our section were just plain old jars of pickles with a couple sliced up on a plate. Some had a bit of rag tied around the top of the jar, or handmade labels. Ours definitely had the most style.

42
The Fair

The Pioneer Fair instructions said to be by our display at 10:30 for judging, so we headed back fifteen minutes early. Principal Lebonsky stood in front of our table, looking down at the *escabeche*. She didn't look up when I walked over, but she sighed the way people do when they know someone is watching.

"I thought we had decided that you'd be entering pickled eggs into the competition, Ben." I gave up all thoughts of escape and moved toward the table. She looked like the *escabeche* smelled. I mean, it did, but she was really making an effort to make that bad-smell face.

"We did. But . . . they didn't turn out like we hoped."

"Well, did you follow my recipe?" She cocked her head and fake-smiled. She didn't blink while she waited for an answer. I broke eye contact and looked around. The pickle makers had split. When we signed in, the Pioneer Fair people had said, "a group representative should be present to offer tastings and share information." I guess that was me.

"We did, I mean, we thought we did. I guess we got the recipe wrong."

"How can you bungle pickled eggs?" Principal Lebonsky's bottom lip turned and puckered like dried fruit. "I gave you a very simple recipe, Ben." I saw Frank and Bean heading into the Colonist Craft Coliseum. Oliver looked away when I spotted him and pretended to be totally fascinated with some dried apple ring wreaths at the other end of the aisle.

"I expected you to provide an authentic example of what local pioneers might have made," she said.

"This *is* authentic," I said. I wished that we had just brought the plastic eggs that Hector had switched for the real ones. I cleared my throat. "Maybe not for your forefathers, but for mine. And a lot of other kids at school. I looked it up." Principal Lebonsky didn't interrupt, so I kept talking. "European settlers pickled things like cucumbers and eggs. Other stuff, too, like watermelons and beets. But not all of the pioneers were from Europe. People came from all over, including Mexico. They needed a way to preserve what grew in their gardens for the winter, too, so they made *escabeche*." I pointed to the article.

"Interesting," Principal Lebonsky said. "I'm impressed,

Ben. It's not what I expected from your League of Pickle Makers."

"It was a surprise for us, too, Principal Lebonsky. I didn't know there were Mexicans here back then." I could feel my heart beating all the way to the top of my head. "But there were, and they probably ate this. If the judges don't think that's authentic, that's their problem. But we know it is."

"You're right, Ben," she said. "You've done your research and collaborated with your pickle-making peers. It is certainly not what we discussed, but I respect the value that you've placed on historical tradition. I trust you'll be able to answer any questions that the judging panel may have?"

I nodded.

"Very well. Good luck." Principal Lebonsky walked on to make sure more Fountain Point exhibits were up to her standards. Oliver, Bean, and Frank walked toward our table like they'd been waiting for the very second that the coast was clear, which of course they had. Leo Saylor ran over from the other direction.

"Just wait until you guys see what we've got planned. It's going to be awesome!" Leo said. He ran down the aisle before we could even ask what he was talking about. Sienna came from the other direction.

"Hey, is your dad here?" I said.

"No, he said he had to work," she said. Her face got

blotchy and it looked like she had chewed off her lip gloss. She walked away to watch a woman knead dough.

We stood together at the table and waited for the judges. I snacked on more *escabeche* and chips. It wasn't like we were going to run out, but I stopped when I could see the judges coming down the aisle. There were three of them. Two men and a woman. I knew that they were the judges because they were dressed up and looked important. And they all wore big blue ribbons that said "JUDGE" in gold letters. They leaned down to inspect some bread. I watched them closely, but I still jumped when the woman judge screamed.

43 No Blue Ribbon

After the judge screamed, she jumped back and smacked at her hair. And her chest. The other two judges tried to help, but then one of them started smacking at his shirt the same way. People moved toward them, and we went, too.

"What's happening?" I asked a guy by the table of dehydrated fruits.

"Bugs," he said. "Looks like there were cockroaches in the bread." He covered up his dried fruit with a big sheet of plastic wrap. I heard kids screaming in other parts of the gym, too. Then a nasty brown bug jumped on my shoulder. I only had time to notice his beady little eyes before he jumped off and into the *escabeche*. I tried to scoop him out, but there were already two more there. I really, really hoped that they hadn't been there while I was snacking. I was having flan flashbacks. Crunchy, nasty, flan. With legs.

I couldn't think about it. I couldn't *not* think about it. The bug that jumped on my shoulder just hung out on a tomatillo, but another one swam in the vinegar. The third bug crawled underneath a piece of onion, and my stomach clenched.

I bent over and grabbed the table. My brain spun with bugs and food. Food and bugs. I tried to think happy thoughts, but it didn't stop my stomach from lurching. Frank crouched down beside me.

"Status update, Ben. Are you all right?"

"No, I'm not. I'm gonna puke," I said.

"You. Must. Chill. Take a deep breath," he said.

"What are those? Roaches?!"

"Don't think about them," Frank said. "Listen. Breathe. Deep breath."

"I really, really hate roaches, Frank," I said.

I took a deep breath and smelled the *escabeche*. I wondered if I had swallowed any bugs. I don't think I'd even notice with the crunchy chip. Another roach jumped on my face. His creepy little legs tickled my cheek. And then I lost it. And by *it*, I mean the oatmeal and toast that I had for breakfast and all of the *escabeche* and chips I had just eaten. I lost it all over the cowboy tablecloth. It looked like someone spilled a vegetable corn chip smoothie. And it smelled even worse.

I stumbled back and sat against the bleachers. I tried to ignore the screaming and yelling. I felt something land on my leg, but I just brushed it off without looking. I heard someone else gag, and I almost threw up again. Someone brought me a wet paper towel. I opened my eyes. Bean was using a curled-up workbook to whack any bugs that jumped on our table. Oliver said he was going to hurl if he had to look at my upchuck anymore, so Frank scooped everything up and carried it to the trash.

"Be careful with the punch bowl!" I called out, and he nodded. Principal Lebonsky's voice came over the P.A. system.

"ATTENTION PIONEER FAIR VISITORS AND EXHIBITORS. THE FOUNTAIN POINT PIONEER FAIR IS HEREBY CANCELED DUE TO UNFORSEEN

PROBLEMS. PLEASE MAKE YOUR WAY TO THE EXITS SO THAT THE SOURCE OF THE DISTURBANCE CAN BE IDENTIFIED AND CONTAINED."

Sienna squatted down in front of me.

"I'm so sorry, Ben," she said.

"It's all right. I'm starting to feel better." I tried to talk without breathing, just in case I had vomit breath.

"Come on, guys. We have to split," Bean said. She held the empty punch bowl, but everything else was in the trash. I felt a little woozy when I stood up, but I knew it would be better if I could make it outside. Sienna and I followed Frank, Bean, and Oliver toward the doors. We passed Principal Lebonsky and Rick moving back toward our table. Then we saw Ms. Ruiz.

"This stinks, guys," Ms. Ruiz said. I thought she was talking about me, but she gestured back toward the fair. "You all must be so disappointed." She moved forward like she wanted to hug me, but then she changed her mind. She took her punch bowl and said we'd regroup later.

"I can't stand cockroaches. You know, I ate one once. By accident," I said. I could see bugs everywhere, but I tried to squint to make them blurry.

"I know. But, they're crickets," Sienna said. "There are thousands of crickets. I'm so, so sorry."

"Are you sure they're crickets?" One landed on my hand and I shook it off. I looked for Sienna, but she was lost in the crowd. Leo was beside me, looking really bummed out.

"Hey, man," I said. "Are you all right?"

"Yeah," he said. "I'm just bummed about the fair getting cancelled. We had a really cool lassoing demonstration planned."

"You're in the lassoing club?" I said.

"Yeah." Leo sighed. "Maybe next year."

We finally got to the doors, but something was slowing everyone down. I stood behind a woman with a sheep on a leash and her arms full of yarn. I tried not to bump the sheep. *Please, no more bugs*, I thought. I couldn't stay in the gym any longer. I pushed through the crowd. I didn't know what was keeping people in the gym, but whatever it was, I wasn't interested. Nothing could stop me from getting outside.

I was wrong. I did stop. I stopped to read the poster boards hung on each side of the door that said:

Special Pioneer Fair wildlife
compliments of the P.T.A.

Finally it dawned on me how Sienna knew that the bugs were crickets.

Another Announcement

I told my parents about the upchuck for sympathy popsicles. I emailed Frank, Bean, and Oliver. So when Sienna showed up at school on Monday morning, the four of us were waiting outside by the fountain.

"Why'd you do it, Sienna?" I asked but she just glared at me. "Is it so bad being here instead of Colorado that you had to ruin it for everybody?" No answer.

"Did you just join the club so you could mess it up?" Bean said. Sienna still didn't answer, but her eyes got watery and she sniffled.

"I just wanted to do it, all right? I thought it would be fun," she said.

"I guess you didn't puke," I said. "It wasn't fun."

"Sorry." She chewed her lip.

"How many bugs were there, anyway?" Oliver said.

"Three thousand," Sienna said. "A little less. Some were dead in the box when I got to the gym."

"Whoa," Frank said. "Where does one procure three thousand crickets?"

"That pet store on Ninth. They sell crickets to feed lizards and stuff," Sienna said. "I bought them all."

"Inspiring," Frank said.

"Where'd you get the money?" Bean said.

"My dad sent me forty bucks in a card to say he wasn't coming to visit," Sienna said. "He said to buy myself something nice."

"And you went with crickets? Not bad, Taylor!" Bean said. She looked impressed. "Maybe I need a Human vs. Bug site! Just think, Ben, if I'd thought to bring my camera you could have been my first video!"

"Shut up, Bean. Did you see the P.T.A. signs? It said we did it," I said.

"That is messed up," Oliver said, and shook his head.

Sienna cried. She wasn't making any noise, but her cheeks were wet and her eye makeup got all smudgy. I wanted to feel bad for her. I did. But, I just couldn't. She might have ruined everything. I turned away and watched the babies pour water, not a bubble in sight. The bell rang, Ms. Ruiz got there, and she pushed us all into the classroom. We sat on one side of the class, and Sienna sat on the other.

Ms. Ruiz was explaining about how our government and

constitution is based on the old Greek way when the P.A. zapped and we heard Principal Lebonsky clear her throat.

"Good morning, students." She talked in a normal voice, so they must have figured out that there was nothing wrong with the intercom. "I hope those of you who were unfortunate enough to have been at the Pioneer Fair during the . . . disturbance . . . over the weekend have recovered sufficiently for your studies. I would like to put an end to rumors that Fountain Point is infested with cockroaches. Some children placed a great number of common brown field CRICKETS in the gymnasium with NO regard for the feelings of their fellow students and Pioneer Fair exhibitors. Mrs. Wimple's pottery wheel did not suffer permanent damage, thankfully, when it was pushed over by overzealous bug squashers." Principal Lebonsky paused. Someone giggled, but Ms. Ruiz shushed us. "BUT, our school district superintendent was present at the fair, along with many members of our school board, and that is not the impression we wanted to make for Fountain Point. Many of our students lost their hard work when it was contaminated and ultimately wasted." The microphone crackled. Nobody spoke. "One fine exhibit in particular was ruined when a Fountain Point student felt sickened enough by the crickets to vomit upon his own display." Oh, sheep. Heads swiveled around to look at me. Maggie Rubio laughed. Word had gotten around then. Good to know.

"I made it clear that this type of activity would not be tolerated. My sources have informed me—"

I tried to stare down at the sweat marks my hands were making on my desk. I did not look at Hector, but others did.

"—that our recent string of hijinks can be traced to an organized group of students who find these types of activities amusing. Therefore, while faculty committees and meetings will continue as scheduled, I regret to inform you that ALL EXTRACURRICULAR ENRICHMENT WILL BE SUSPENDED UNTIL THESE EVENTS CEASE TO OCCUR. This includes ALL STUDENT CLUBS, ORGANIZATIONS, AND TEAMS." She knew the intercom wasn't broken, but she yelled anyway. "Baseball tryouts are cancelled INDEFINITELY. Perhaps those responsible will realize the effect their actions are having on their peers and do the right thing. This is a matter of INDIVIDUAL ACCOUNTABILITY. This is not open for discussion. There will be consequences when the group is identified. Anyone with information will find that my office door is open. Have a good day."

The intercom gave a static zap when it turned off, and the classroom filled with buzzing whispers. Maggie Rubio played for the volleyball team and she looked like she was about to cry, but just about everyone else looked mad. Even the kids who weren't in any clubs or sports.

Bugs or no bugs, Principal Lebonsky had gone too far.

A New Pickle

We tried to meet in the lab after school on Thursday, but the door was locked.

"How about Lupe's?" Oliver said.

"Too risky," Frank said. "We shouldn't be overheard."

"I think it will be all right," I said. "Things have been slow, and people don't usually eat in the middle of the afternoon."

Five minutes later the pickle makers were in our usual booth and I was in the kitchen getting some chips, salsa, and guacamole. My mom and dad weren't around, so we had full soda machine access. If things had been better in the league, it would have been a party, but I didn't feel like celebrating.

We all just sat there. Nobody talked. Maybe meeting at the restaurant was a bad idea. One loose cricket, and someone could call the state health inspector. Or one could crawl into the food. I got up and got sodas for everyone and brought them back to the table. I banged the tray down.

"You know what, Sienna? Maybe you shouldn't even be here. You obviously don't care about the club," I said. She didn't look at me, but she looked at Oliver. That just made me more mad.

"Look, Ben"—Oliver held his hands up—"I'm sorry you ralphed all over our display, but she didn't think all that would happen. Did you?" Sienna shook her head and sniffed. "Just because you ate one before, how was she to know that they'd make you do *that*?" Like because she didn't predict that three thousand crickets attacking would make me lose my breakfast, everything was fine. I couldn't believe it.

"Crickets have bigger back legs than cockroaches do," Oliver said. "If you just looked closer you would've been able to tell they weren't roaches."

"I wasn't inspecting their legs," I said through gritted teeth. "I was trying not to look at them at all." Sienna blew her nose on a napkin. "This club was the best thing to happen to me since we started middle school, and now it's all over. The next three years are going to stink!" I felt a lump in my throat, and my lip quivered. If I puked and cried in the same week, I might as well just transfer to a new school. Nobody said anything.

"Don't just try to make her feel bad. We have to think how to fix things," Oliver said.

"How are we going to fix it? She pretty much killed the P.T.A. and all of the other extracurricular stuff, too!" I said. "Forget it, this meeting is over." I cleared off the table and stormed out of the restaurant. I was supposed to stay and help with dinner, but first I wanted them to know how mad I was. The pickle makers followed me out and found me right in front standing on the sidewalk. I should have gone around the block or something.

"Ben, please. You guys listen to me for a second." Sienna grabbed my arm. "I think that saying we can't meet is unconstitutional. We were just studying that kind of stuff at my old school before we moved. It's in the First Amendment, and it's called the right to peaceably assemble."

"I don't think that applies to kids," I said.

"There's no reason it wouldn't," Bean said. "It says something like people can be in groups, as long as they're not fighting and stuff, right?"

"Right," Sienna said. "So, we should be able to meet for pickle making. Or volleyball, or whatever."

Oliver said they were both crazy, and that kids don't have any rights.

"Well, we should," Frank said. "And how better to get rights, than to *demand* rights!"

I wasn't ready to forgive and forget with Sienna, but the idea of doing something, to show them that we couldn't be pushed around like this . . . I liked it. Principal Lebonsky couldn't stop everybody from doing all the stuff they loved just because we messed up. It shouldn't be like that, but I could see how we might be able to fix it.

"How bad do you think the kids at school want to get their teams back?" I asked.

"Bad. I saw a couple of the soccer players crying in the bathroom," Bean said. "Over *soccer*."

"What if we protested?" I said.

"Who would care?" Oliver said.

"I'm not talking about just us. The pickle makers aren't the only ones who matter," I said. "I mean the entire school. I think *everybody* would protest."

"Why? Kids that aren't in any clubs don't care," Oliver said.

"Yes they do," Frank said. "People can choose what they want. Who they want to do things with. Even if it's not a club. It's about freedom."

"Could we get the word out for everybody to meet up?" Bean said.

"Maybe, but what good would that do?" Oliver said.

"It could get the clubs back," I said. "It would show

Principal Lebonsky that she can't just change things because she's mad. That we're old enough to decide what we want to do for ourselves. That's what she said at the beginning of the year—we're older now and we are supposed to be responsible for our choices. We can't if she won't let us."

"We can do it. I know we can," Sienna said. She was done crying. "I started this. I need to fix it. Can you guys help me?"

We didn't need to vote or anything. We were all excited. Oliver said it would be his most important role yet.

"We need to protest for our right to assemble, right?" I said. "We could tell everyone to come with their teams, for a sit-in or whatever."

"My parents went to a protest rally when they were knocking down some old building in Denver for condos. Back when they were still together." Sienna said. She'd cried her makeup off, but it kind of just made her prettier.

"We could do it Monday morning at the assembly," I said. "It's perfect!"

"What assembly?"

"Pat announced it the other day. There's something on Monday morning about eating more colorful foods, or something," I said. Frank and Oliver looked like they were on board, but Bean still frowned.

"How could we tell everybody in time?" Bean asked, and I swear to cheese Frank busted out a calculator.

"It won't work—the seventh and eighth graders are never going to want to do it if they think sixth graders put it together," Oliver said.

"Nobody will have to know. Six of us each tell six people. They each tell six people. *They* each tell six people. It will spread through the whole school and no one will know where it started," Frank said. He glanced down at his calculator. "I estimate that the entire school would be informed in under three hours."

"What if the same people get told twice?"

"So?" I said. "Tell everybody to tell new people. At least the people in their clubs or on their teams."

We decided to have a backup plan, just in case everyone didn't hear. Oliver wanted to put signs up on the bathroom mirrors, but Frank said that a teacher or somebody might go into the bathroom during the day and see the sign.

"Nah, when teachers go in the student restroom for something they always leave the door open. If we put the sign on the back of the door, nobody will see it but kids," Frank said. He was right. Even when Rick went in there to mop, the first thing he did was prop the door open with the bucket.

And then Frank suggested a way to make the protest especially awesome from something he'd seen online. The League of Pickle Makers had a plan, but only one day before the weekend. And the assembly was first thing on Monday.

We got to work right away.

Getting the Word Out

I went around the bathrooms right after school ended on Friday to check the signs, and they were all still taped up. It was a pretty genius idea to put them on the backs of the doors, but here's the really great part. When we told kids about the assembly, we said that we had heard from

somebody else and we were supposed to pass it on, like we were just links in the chain. Nobody knew where it started, and the P.T.A. stayed undercover. Everything was smooth as butter.

It didn't even take three hours to get the word out, like Frank had estimated. I knew things were in motion because kids I didn't even know were stopping me between classes and at lunch to whisper protest instructions. I said I'd be there. I didn't even have to pretend that I was surprised and excited. I was—surprised, I mean—even though we were the ones who planned it. I couldn't believe how enthusiastic everybody was. Frank was right about students being fed up. I passed Principal Lebonsky on my way out of school. She looked like she was in a huff, but no more than normal. I said goodbye, and she just nodded.

Now all we had to do was wait.

Waiting

Over the weekend I thought about how we could have planned it better. I didn't know if what we had done would be enough, but I did get a bunch of emails, including two from seventh graders and four from eighth graders, making sure I knew about it. A boy I didn't know eating lunch at Lupe's mouthed "Do . . . you . . . know . . . about . . . Monday?" I nodded, and he gave a thumbs-up under the table. Maybe it would work, but maybe it would bomb. Waiting until Monday was worse than waiting for Christmas.

48 We Assemble

The League of Pickle Makers/P.T.A. sat smack dab in the middle of the bleachers so we could see everything that happened. We took up half a row about twenty feet up from the podium. I made eye contact with Hector when he came into the gym, but he looked away. And then he sat down in the middle of the second row. Excited kids filled the benches around us.

Everybody seemed really pumped up. The gym was extra loud, like a basketball game or something, not a lecture on eating more vegetables. The bleachers were full of kids all talking at once until Principal Lebonsky started with the one-two-three-eyes-on-me claps. Everybody quieted down, but the gym still seemed to be buzzing. She introduced a lady with a picture of smiling broccoli on her T-shirt. She listed every food she could think of that was a rainbow color for thirty minutes. I was fine with the tomatoes and raspberries, but by the time she got to the grand finale of eggplants and purple kale, I was ready to jump out of my seat. I wasn't the only one. She finished and the whole gym cheered. The vegetable woman looked really proud, like she'd convinced us all to give up chips and candy forever. When she left, I felt relieved that she wouldn't know why everyone was *really* so excited.

"All right, children. Settle down," Principal Lebonsky said. Bean growled and a few kids around us made faces. I wasn't the only one who doesn't like it when she calls us "children." She tapped her fingers on the podium while she waited for the gym to get quiet. "I want to start off with a hearty congratulations to our extracurricular enrichment groups that worked so hard preparing exhibits for our Pioneer Fair. I only had time to see the displays from our Knotty Knitters, the League of Pickle Makers, and the Beaver Bakers, but they all certainly met expectations." I'm not sure that was a compliment, but everybody clapped really loud. I think they clapped with protest excitement, not pickle and yarn enthusiasm. Principal Lebonsky cleared her throat. "Even though our judges did not get the chance to make evaluations for the competitions, each of you are winners because many pioneers succeeded and did not succumb to starvation and fever."

It was a little awkward, but we clapped for the pioneers.

"I'm going to succumb to starvation before she's done wagging her finger at us," Bean whispered.

"Despite your potential talents for the Pioneer Fair, you all know that having organized groups is a privilege, not a right," Principal Lebonsky said. The crowd muttered. "Each of you needs to bear the torch of student responsibility. When I know with *absolute* certainty that the senseless shenanigans have ended, then I will *consider* allowing extracurricular activities and sports play again." The buzz from the crowd got louder. She held up some character cards, which I'd only ever seen her use with Hector. I thought she would pass them out, but she just read some quotes from Benjamin Franklin and one of the Roosevelts. You couldn't really hear her when she said we were excused to go back to class. She leaned closer to the microphone and said it again.

Nobody moved.

She did another of her one-two-three-eyes-on-me claps. Frank had said she would. It was our cue. The gym grew quiet as people realized that this was the part that they had been waiting for. It was time. Everyone stopped talking and froze in place.

Bean had her hands up like she was in the middle of describing something. The girl at the end of our row froze while tying her shoe. Leo Saylor looked like a statue putting his backpack on. Hector was turned around in his seat looking straight at me. I tried to read his expression, but he was too far away.

I heard a couple of girls in the back giggling. And then, from under the bleachers, a cricket chirped.

"Fountain Point football, FOREVER!" one of the football players yelled, and the other football players jumped up, yelling and clapping. The instructions we had given out said to freeze in place for two minutes. I didn't think it had been two minutes yet, but I'm glad that they were excited. The football captain gestured and the team, who'd been kind of spread across the bleachers, worked their way down to sit at center court and start the flash mob. We all unfroze and clapped. The kids, I mean. The grown-ups just looked confused.

"You can all just return to class. *Right now*," Principal Lebonsky said again. Maggie Rubio stood up, but she just moved down to the gym floor with her volleyball team. The chess club went next. They all wore chess club T-shirts with the big horse piece on the front. I wondered if it was just coincidence and then the dance club stood up and took their sweatshirts off to show those crazy blue sparkly leotards they have. They all went down the bleacher stairs to the gym floor, too. Dancing.

A few teachers got up and tried to talk to their students on the floor, but the kids wouldn't budge. Some wouldn't even look at the teachers. Then the science club, the band, and the drama club moved down. Oliver pulled a top hat and cape out of his backpack and put them on with a twirl. He winked at us and headed down to join the other theater people on the gym floor. Oliver wasn't the only one dressed up. A seventh grader pulled a jester hat and some balls out from under his sweatshirt and juggled. Some kid ran in late to the gym with a Fountain point shirt stretched over a beaver costume that may or may not have come from Lee's. They were all singing a song about a parade passing that I could only guess came from *Hello, Dolly!* The cheerleaders hopped down the bleacher stairs shaking pom-poms and *woohoo*ing. Some of the clubs that didn't have uniforms wore matching shirts. Some of the kids that were in more than one thing wore clothes to match a couple of groups and sat between them. I guessed the kids with ropes were the lasso club. Leo was with them, but he had a basketball jersey on, too. Almost everybody was out of the bleachers. They stomped and pounded the gym floor with their fists. The whole gym rumbled. Bean elbowed me.

"Somebody better explain to me what you all think you are doing," Principal Lebonsky said. Nobody said anything. Kids who didn't have any clubs were forming groups to sit and protest with. Our row was some of the last kids in the stands. Bean nudged me again and we moved down the stairs to join the others on the gym floor.

"Who is responsible for this foolishness? I DEMAND AN ANSWER!" Principal Lebonsky's voice boomed through the microphone. I locked eyes with Hector, and stopped. He still sat in his seat and I could see his expression now. He looked petrified.

Principal Lebonsky noticed Hector's face, too. "Hector Lebonsky! Do you have anything to do with this, this, *anarchy*?" Hector's head whipped around to look at his grandma. I think he wanted to say something, but he couldn't. "This will *not* be tolerated!" she said. I knew what I had to do. My feet moved toward the stage while my heart tried to keep going to the center of the gym floor. My brain just screamed. The rest of the pickle makers seemed confused, but they kept going toward the free-throw line like we'd planned. Principal Lebonsky took a couple of steps toward Hector, and I saw my chance. I darted behind her and grabbed the microphone. Hector looked even more horrified. Principal Lebonsky tried to grab the microphone back, but I jumped out of the way and faced the students on the gym floor. The bleachers were deserted, except for Hector and a few kids. Some of them looked confused, and some looked like they might be protesting the protest.

I'd never talked into a microphone in my entire life, which would explain why the first noise I made totally sounded like a squeegee. I would have rather touched the dry ice again than stand at the podium with a microphone, but my feet didn't move.

"I'm Ben Diaz. I am the president of the P.T.A." I made

eye contact with Principal Lebonsky to make sure she understood. I swear her eyes flashed red. Her face got red, too. She reached out to grab the microphone back, but I moved away. I looked at Ms. Ruiz , but she looked almost as mad as Principal Lebonsky so I looked at the pickle makers. The clapping and stomping stopped and the gym grew so quiet I could hear myself breathing over the P.A. "We, the students of Fountain Point, are exercising our constitutional right to assemble. We want our extracurricular activities back!" I don't think I said it very loud, but people clapped. Really. The crowd went wild, just like they say at baseball games. It dawned on people what I'd said and what it meant, and *everybody* cheered. Bean *woot*ed and Oliver put his fingers in his mouth and did one of those loud whistles. Sienna yelled, "Yay, Ben!" Frank looked horrified. I looked back at Hector, who still sat in the bleachers with his head in his hands. Everybody else looked happy. It was probably one of the coolest moments I will ever have. The whole school smiled at me.

I looked back at Ms. Ruiz and she was shaking her head, but even she was smiling a little bit. I think she might've liked the bit about the constitution.

Principal Lebonsky, however, wasn't smiling. Her eyes weren't red anymore, but her face looked like a stop sign.

"Ben, did you do this alone?" she hissed.

"No! No, he didn't!" Hector yelled and stood up. My heart started thumping against my ribs again. If she didn't know it was the League of Pickle Makers, there was no reason to tell her.

"Hector, don't—" I said. Hector wrestled me for the microphone. I tried to hold on to it but my hands were sweaty and it slipped out like I handed it to him. I thought about punching him in the mouth before he could rat out the rest of the league, but I knew I never could.

"Hi. I'm Hector. Hector Lebonsky. Yes, that's my

grandma." He gestured impatiently to Principal Lebonsky. He talked fast. "But, I helped him. I totally helped him. Ben and me. We did it all together." Hector swallowed, and I could hear the gulp. "If you think about it, he couldn't have done all that alone. So we did it together." Hector said. All I could do was stare.

"Hector," Principal Lebonsky sputtered. "*Why?*"

"We're friends. And sometimes you just have to do stuff for the fun of it," Hector said, and smiled. Principal Lebonsky rubbed her eyes. The League of Pickle Makers seemed to be arguing. Everybody else stood up and clapped.

Principal Lebonsky grabbed my arm, and then she grabbed Hector's arm. She marched us off of the stage. It just made the crowd whoop louder.

"To my office. *Right. Now*," she growled, and pushed us forward. The gym doors slammed behind us, but I could still hear the cheering.

The Jig Is Up

Principal Lebonsky put us in her office and told us to "wait right there" while she straightened up the "hijinks in the gym." I heard her say something that sounded like "water bell" on the way out. She was gone for a really, really long time.

Hector didn't say a word to me. He ignored me and stared at an apple mug full of pens on Principal Lebonsky's desk. She also has an apple paper clip holder, an apple notepad, and the apple tape dispenser my family had bought her for Christmas, back when I still called her Betty.

We almost got away with everything. If I'd just kept walking and sat with the rest of the P.T.A., Principal Lebonsky would've never known what caused her students to revolt. And then Hector had to get involved. That just made it worse, and by worse I mean that Principal Lebonsky might actually explode.

"Why did you do that?" I asked him, but he wouldn't even look at me. He just looked mad. And scared.

Principal Lebonsky came back to her office, shut the door, and walked over to her desk. She set a different apple mug full of coffee on top of a pad of detention slips and stared us down for over a minute before she sat down.

"You arranged this? This *protest*?" I nodded. "The soap in the fountain, the dry ice in the gym, and that disgusting business at the Pioneer Fair? You are responsible for *all* of it? Am I clear on this?"

"No, not the fair, that was—never mind. Yes," I said.

"You created such a horrific spectacle with the insects, you caused your own self to become sick." Principal Lebonsky shook her head. I was almost still mad enough at Sienna to sell her out, but I didn't.

"Yes," I said. "I did it. I am disgusting."

"I am ashamed of you, Ben Diaz. Your parents didn't raise you to be so disorderly. You should know better," she said. I wanted to tell her that my parents didn't raise me to be pushed around, either, but I didn't. "What exactly does P.T.A. stand for? Pickles, Tomfoolery, and, and ANARCHY?!"

"No, it's—"

"And, YOU, Hector Lebonsky! You knew about this. You took part," Principal Lebonsky said. Hector didn't say anything. He looked green.

"Principal Lebonsky, Hector didn't—"

"Silence, Ben. That is enough!" She glared at Hector for a long time. He seemed to be shivering. "Hector, I'm not sure what part you took in all of this, but we will deal with it later at home," she said. I wondered how many new character cards she would make. Maybe she'd pin them to his clothes. She gave Hector a whole lot of stink eye before turning back to me. "Hector, go to class," she said. "We'll discuss this tonight." Hector spun out of his chair and left before I could say anything. Principal Lebonsky sat forward and sighed.

"Out with it, Benjamin. Let's get everything straight before I call your parents."

I told her the only thing I could.

50 Repercussions

The phone rang a lot after school let out until my dad turned the ringer off. I wasn't allowed to answer it. I wasn't allowed to check my email, either. Or be online at all, so I couldn't go to the Pickles Forever website. I couldn't play video games, or watch TV. When my mom and dad went to the restaurant, I went with them every time. The dishwasher quit and moved to Texas, so the timing was pretty bad that way. I got to do all the honors.

"We're proud of you for standing up for what you believe in, but there need to be *consecuencias por los problemas en la escuela*," my dad said. Consequences for the trouble at school. And the money they were saving by not paying a dishwasher could go in my college fund.

I smelled like dish detergent all the time. I dreamed that the halls at school were full of half-eaten food. Horrible.

I thought about what I would tell the P.T.A. when my parents let me hang out with them again, but I didn't have to wait that long. They were all waiting down on the sidewalk outside my building before school on Monday.

"So, what happened?" Sienna grabbed my sleeve. "What's happening with the club?" I shook her off and walked toward school.

"Tell us what she said, rat butt." Bean would have shot lasers out of her eyes, if she was a laser-shooting robot. A robot with rage. A lot of the time she had a look on her face like she thought about smacking me, but she looked a little more wound up now. Her control knob was turned all the way up to Clobber. "Are we going to get in trouble when we get to school?"

"Nope," I said. "Not at all. She doesn't know you were involved."

"You took all the credit?" Frank looked disgusted.

"He didn't take the credit, he took the heat. You didn't have to do that," Sienna said. She hugged me. "I don't know how we can make it up to you."

"I don't know *why* we should make it up to you," Bean mumbled. "If it wasn't for Ben, we'd still have secret identities."

Sienna ignored her.

"What's she going to do to you?"

"Detention. I have to help Rick clean after school for a month. Then I have to go help at the restaurant," I said. "I have to get up extra early for homework. Not a drop of free time." Frank winced.

"Sorry, man," he said. I shrugged. It could have been a lot worse.

"What about Hector?" Bean said. "What did she do to that lying, credit-taking worm?"

I could remind them that Hector had saved them from getting busted, but I didn't think they were ready to hear it. And that might just remind them that it was me that almost got them busted. "She thought Hector was involved, but I told her he wasn't. He just wanted to help." I looked at Bean. "And he's not a worm."

It wasn't hard to convince Principal Lebonsky that I had done it all by myself. I think she wanted to believe that Hector behaved. Otherwise, she'd have to admit that her character cards were a bust.

"She said all the clubs and teams could start meeting again next week." Oliver clapped and Frank pumped his fist in the air.

"The show must go on!" Oliver yelled. "I can't wait to tell the cast and crew."

"All right, time for school, you monkey butts," Bean said. She turned down the sidewalk, and Frank and Oliver followed.

"You guys go ahead," I said. "I'm going to wait for Hector." Bean rolled her eyes, and Oliver shook his head, but Frank nodded and Sienna smiled at me.

"See you at school," she said.

I watched Hector come out of our building. He looked behind him to make sure his grandma wasn't coming, and then he tossed his protein bar in a trash can. He saw me and smiled. Then he scowled.

"I wanted to say thanks for what you did at the assembly. It was nice of you to protect the club," I said. Hector scoffed.

"I didn't do it for those meatballs," he said. "I did it for you."

"What?"

"It's true," he said. "I think I get why you've been doing what you've been doing," he said. "Except the bugs. That was gross."

"That wasn't me. That was Sienna," I said. He looked up.

"Really? The new girl?"

I nodded. Hector shook his head.

"Nasty. But, she's kind of cute."

"Yeah?" I said. Hector just shrugged, but he was blushing. I smiled. "I think you're right. You know, you can throw away the eggs. We don't need them anymore." Hector waved me off.

"I threw them away two days ago," he said. "I was this close to hiding them in your room so they would get all foul before you found them."

"That would have been awful," I said. "But kind of funny, too."

When I got home from helping at the restaurant that night I snuck onto the computer before bed. I went straight to my email, where I found new messages from Agent Fix-it, Agent 008, Agent Super, and Agent Snow. They all said the same thing.

Pickle.

But then my mom busted me before I could go to the website.

When Oliver, Frank, Bean, and Sienna met me at the janitorial supply closet after school, I figured they had just stopped by to thank me for sacrificing myself. But, that wasn't it. They had turned themselves in. They told Principal Lebonsky that it had been the League of Pickle Makers all along, so now we were all extra janitors for the month. They didn't have to do that, but it was pretty awesome that they did. Like, *really* awesome.

Rick told us about a time in school when he put a whoopee cushion on his teacher's chair. That's about a zero for originality, but he seemed pretty pleased with himself so we acted like it was brilliant. He let us off the detention hook a week early.

The end. Mostly.

You Can Call It an Epilogue if You Want

The League of Pickle Makers still meets on Thursdays. We use the website a lot and hang out together at school. It's funny, because when we started at Fountain Point, I wouldn't have guessed I'd be friends with any of them. Frank came over to play video games last week, and he brought a couple of seventh graders. They want to join the league. We'll see. Oliver is teaching Sienna how to play guitar, and he talked Bean into joining the drama club and trying out for the next play. We stopped pickling after the *escabeche*, but then Principal Lebonsky said we couldn't collect club funding unless we were "actively pursuing the mastery of preservation." So we made pickled eggs again. They weren't terrible.

We don't really need the money that much. I get paid now when I help in the restaurant, and Sienna's dad sends checks regularly that she likes to use, um, creatively. We made her swear a solemn vow never to go rogue again. Or buy bugs. At least without asking us first. Frank started a business setting up websites for some of the other clubs so that they could have secret sections, too. He donates some of the money from that when we need supplies. Frank and Bean are working on a project for a contest to win a trip to the International Spy Museum. They won't tell me what it is, but they do seem to know a lot of details about conversations they weren't around for.

After detention ended I had a talk with my mom and dad. They're going to try and ask me to work in the restaurant instead of telling me to, unless they're in a real pinch or something. I have so much free time, I'm thinking about starting another club. Just kidding. Sort of.

Oh yeah, I found out something interesting. Leo Saylor quit junior baseball AND young golfers without telling his dad. He would just go to the library after school until his dad came to pick him up. Sometimes he napped in the big cozy chair in the back, but he read a lot, too. Leo said he never had any time to read before, but since he quit going to baseball and golfing he's read all of the Harry Potter books. Twice.

His dad finally busted him on Wednesday, but the *really* interesting part is that Hector knew about it all along! Leo told him the first day he skipped, and Hector never told anybody. There is definitely hope for that dude.

Frank did a lot of work on the Pickles Forever website, and it's huge. There's a message board where we can answer questions and give prank advice. You know, just in case you need any help.

Word spread pretty quickly that the five of us were behind everything. People said that they couldn't believe that a group of sixth graders did it all. I saw Oliver autographing somebody's missing sense of humor flyer. It's not just Fountain Point anymore. We get messages from all over. A ninth grader in Missouri had a ghost prank where he started a rumor about a ghost haunting a specific locker that nobody was using. He misted the inside with spray bottles of milk so that there would be a "smell of evil" when it started to go bad.

We've even gone international! A kid in Brisbane, Australia, posted last week to thank us for the plastic-wrapped sink instructions, and he shared another idea for fake ghosts. He stacked up books in the library and left some gobs of goop on the table. Just like in that old movie, *Ghostbusters*. He made the goop out of cornstarch and glue. We didn't do it, but we put it on the website and somebody else at our school did it last week. You wouldn't believe how freaked out people can get from some books on the floor. It's really something. Other kids at our school are doing pranks, and I have no idea who it is. It's just fun to sit back and watch. Principal Lebonsky calls us in for questioning sometimes, but we usually have alibis for whatever happened. It's driving her crazy.

She's tried talking to my parents about "implementing a successful character-building program" with her goofy cards, but they're not buying it.

A seventh grader from Wisconsin posted about stuffing lockers full of Ping-Pong balls, and it's been happening all over Fountain Point. A ninth grader in Albuquerque shared instructions to get shaving foam into somebody's room with an envelope through a crack in the door. I came home from school on Tuesday to find a mountain of foam where my desk used to be. A couple of cans of "Forest Glen Scented" shaving cream and a yellow envelope were taped to the window on the fire escape that I keep cracked open. I'm not sure what a forest glen smells like, but my room smelled like one of those pine tree air fresheners my grandpa hangs in his car. My mom said the smell was an improvement. Hector's room is right below mine with a window on the fire escape, so I'm pretty sure I know who was behind that little trick.

My mom did not even look grateful when I told her that I would clean it up.

So, now you know the whole story. I've probably said too much, but this is exactly how it all went down. Well, I left out one little thing about what happened to Hector when someone put some popping caps under the toilet seats in the boys' bathroom.

That's what friends are for.

Acknowledgments

Making a book takes enough people to fill a small set of bleachers. I have immeasurable gratitude for everyone who has ever supported me as a writer and/or a troublemaker. I remember each of the teachers and librarians who took the time to imprint a love of books, support my writing aspirations, and/or look beyond any trouble I may have caused to nurture the spark of productive-member-of-society potential. I am in your debt.

My family has always been reasonably patient with my shenanigans and supportive of my creative endeavors, and I love them for it.

I appreciate anyone who read drafts of *Pickle* and gave their constructive feedback. I received guidance and support from Peggy King Anderson, Dana Arnim, Martha Brockenbrough, Jordan Brown, Karen Chalupnik, Sara Easterly, Lisa Graff, Grace Lin, Joni Sensel, Jolie Stekly, and Laurie Thompson. And especially Jaime Temairik and Sam Baker. Without their influence, *Pickle* would be profoundly different. And it would stink.

Thank you to the SCBWI tribe for the wisdom, camaraderie, and resources imparted to newbies and pros alike.

Huge hugs and gratitude to my marvelous agent, Sara Crowe. I am so honored to be part of the Crowe's Nest.

Thanks to Tim Probert for making the P.T.A. come to life. And to the whole team at Macmillan and Roaring Brook, especially my editor, Deirdre Langeland—you guys are tops. Thank you for your vision and guidance. And, you know, for making this an actual book.

I am grateful for a dream come true.